# FIGHTER'S SECRET

A. RIVERS

*To Sheridan,*
*For giving your time generously,*
*being generally awesome,*
*and never failing to make me smile.*

## Chapter One

*HARLEY*

I dodge a punch my half-brother throws at me and wish it was this easy to evade the blows life keeps dealing me lately. Seth is twice my size, but also twelve years older and out of practice. Yeah, he might spar with the fighters who train here at Crown MMA Gym —one of Las Vegas's premier homes of professional mixed martial arts—but he hasn't fought in ages. Meanwhile, I've been living and breathing muay thai for years, and it shows.

Here in the cage, I have it all together. I can forget about the way my world has crumbled around me and simply exist in the moment. In fact, it's essential to do so because if I slip out of the present, I might find myself eating one of Seth's famous straight rights. I smirk as I circle him, looking for a weak point, loving the challenge. Most people don't understand my passion for fighting. It's not a typical occupation for a twenty-something woman.

With a quick, practiced motion, I strike, snapping my padded shin out to thud into the inner part of his thigh. He's slow to react, and his leg starts to buckle beneath him. Knowing he'll save himself before he hits the floor, I use his distraction against him and ram my knee into his solar plexus.

*Bam. Got you.*

He recovers before I can take a shot at his head, and wrestles me into a clinch. His arms are like anacondas, so there's no way I can overpower him, which means I need to either bear it out, or outsmart him.

God, I love this—even when I get a noseful of his sweat-soaked shoulder. I haven't sparred with Seth since he was a UFC champion. I've been out of the country for years, but the time apart hasn't changed how it feels to let loose with him like this. It's the way we communicate. The only language we're both fluent in. And now that I'm here, with his support, I'm beginning to feel like the sun is rising on a new day and perhaps everything will turn out all right.

"Lock me up," he grunts, ever the coach.

Maneuvering him into the corner, I wind my leg around his so he can't do anything, and hold on. When the timer shrieks, ending the round, I release him. We bump fists, then I yank one of my gloves off, grab a towel from where it's hanging over the edge of the cage, and mop my face with it. My hair is coming loose, so I wrangle it back into a ponytail.

"You're good," Seth says, his lips pursing as he evaluates me. I wonder what he sees: the baby sister I used to be, or the athlete Thailand turned me into. "But we need to get you grappling sooner rather than later if you're going to win that eight-man eliminator."

I nod, acknowledging what we both know: I'm at a significant disadvantage for my big debut. He's signed me up for my first professional MMA bouts—three in one night. Eight women begin the tournament, and only one emerges as victor. We both want me to be the one left standing, even if our reasons for that differ. He wants the good publicity it'll bring his gym, while I need a win after the month I've had.

The trouble is, all of my professional experience is in muay thai, which is strictly stand-up striking. MMA, with the jiu-jitsu element on the floor, is a completely different beast. That's okay, though. I'm ready for it. I have nothing but time on my hands to prepare. I uprooted my entire life to move back here, and I don't even have a bed to call my own. Seth is loaning me his spare room, but to be honest, I'm not sure how often I'll sleep there. After living on-site at my gym in Thailand, it'll be hard to move into an apartment. I already miss the sun and warmth. Unfortunately, I couldn't stay. Not after what happened.

"Do five rounds on bags, then we'll talk through your training plan."

With that, I'm dismissed. I slip my glove back on and head to one of the heavy bags. After a moment, I feel eyes on my back and turn to find an insanely hot fighter watching me.

*Devon.*

Even his name is sexy. He sends me a wicked grin, then strips off his shirt and starts punching a bag. His brown abs glisten with sweat and shift beneath his skin like he's a sleek panther. But men with abs are nothing new to me, and however yummy he is, he looks like trouble. I don't need any more of that right now. Besides, Seth warned me before I even set foot in the gym, not to hook up with any of his fighters—something about not introducing unnecessary drama—and I know he's made it clear to them that I'm off-limits too.

Turning back to the bag, I take a moment to scope out its size and shape. It's newer than the ones I'm used to. Flashier too. Getting into stance, I throw a jab then a cross, and snap my fists back to my chin. *Always protect the jaw.* Trust me, I learned that lesson fast. I reach out to get a sense of the distance, then back off and slam a kick into it. My shin thumps across the solid fabric, but I hardly feel it. Bags are nothing compared to the dozens of shins that have clashed with my own.

Now that I'm comfortable with the bag, I launch a few combinations. Punches, kicks, knees, elbows. Shortly, the beeper ends the round. I drop to the floor and start doing sit-ups. Not that I have to. The thirty seconds between rounds is technically a break, but I like to make the most of the time I've got.

A face appears above me. Dark eyes and a mischievous smile. I continue my sit-ups, ignoring the way my body reacts to the handsome fighter, tingling in places it shouldn't. I silently reprimand it. A nice smile and a killer physique don't make a man worth my time. Recent experience should tell me that.

"Good form," he says, raking his gaze down my body in a way that brings my nipples to attention. Fortunately, it's impossible to see anything through my thick sports bra.

"Thanks. I try."

He winks. "You succeed."

Oh, my God. He's a flirt. Exactly what I don't need.

The beeper ends the break, and Devon offers me a hand up. I grab it and haul myself to my feet. But something strange happens when we touch. Energy pulses through my body, awakening every nerve until I'm hyperaware of the movement of my skin against his. The instant my feet are steady beneath me, I drop

4

his hand, desperate to end the strange sensation. His eyes catch mine and the way he searches them tells me he felt it too, but far from being discomfited, he seems enthralled. He doesn't return to his bag as I expect. Instead, he wraps an arm around mine, effectively taking it out of commission.

"So how are you settling into Vegas?"

I shrug, irritated with him for getting up in my face with all of his sexiness. "It's fine. It's no Thailand, but there are worse places."

"I bet Seth hasn't given you the grand tour." He cocks his head, and his full lips twitch into a smile. Something twinges inside of me, and I have the insane urge to bite into his lower lip. Shaking my head, I clear the thought. "I'm an excellent tour guide," he continues, "and I happen to be free as soon as training ends. I'll show you around."

"No, thanks. I'm perfectly capable of figuring the city out for myself."

His brows shoot up. "Oh, so that's how you're going to play it?"

"Play what?"

"You're going to pretend you don't feel this thing between us?"

I shake my head, incredulous. "We just met."

He shrugs. "That doesn't mean anything. Some of the world's greatest romances happened in only a few days."

This guy really is trouble. "Didn't Seth give you 'the talk'?"

His grin widens. "I offered to show you around town, that's all. I'd do the same for any other fighter who was new to the area."

"Uh-huh." I glance at the timer and see he's already wasted half of the round. "Listen, I haven't worked out for several days because I've been in transit and I really need to get back into it. Do you mind?"

He releases the bag, but I can tell from his expression that this isn't the end of the conversation. He might be backing off for now, but it's a temporary reprieve. That's fine. I look forward to round two.

"Dev!" Seth yells across the room. "Harley! Less talking, more sparring."

"Me and her?" His smile falters, but he catches it quickly. He wasn't expecting that.

"Come on, then." I raise my fists and challenge him, waiting to see what he'll do. Some guys don't like sparring with a female partner. They get weird about it.

He bumps my gloves and steps back, scanning me in a way that's two-thirds analytical and one-third sexual. He's trying to take me seriously, but can't help checking me out. I resist the urge to roll my eyes. That's such a guy thing to do, and honestly, I hope he underestimates me. Silently, I dare him to.

He moves forward, but he's hesitant and all it takes is a push-kick in the solar plexus to stop him in his tracks. He fires back with a body kick but it's slow and weak. I check it easily and sigh. So this is how it's going to be. He's afraid to hurt me. As if he really could. I'm not some delicate flower, and by the time this round is over, he'll know not to treat me like one.

He throws a half-hearted hook, which I block, and then I step forward and deliver a perfectly placed uppercut to the soft piece of flesh on the underside of his chin. His eyes bulge in shock, but rather than looking annoyed as most men typically do when they're outdone by a woman, he laughs and studies me like I'm the most fascinating thing he's ever seen.

So this is how it feels to be punched in the face by love. I have to say, I kind of like it. I like this girl, too. She's a warrior princess who put Seth on his ass and turned down my invitation without a second thought. Harley Isles isn't going to be easy to win over, but the worthwhile adventures never are. All I know for sure is that I can't wait to learn more about her. To find out what gets under her skin.

Moving forward, I keep my guard up because she packs a lot of power for her size, and clearly has the skills to take down a guy like me if I don't stay on my toes. I fucking love that about her. This time, I throw a fake with my left arm, then as she shields her face, I drop low and land a shot to her gut. Or perhaps I should say her abs, because there's nothing soft about them. They flex beneath my fist and the air gusts from her lungs, but she doesn't crumple or gasp for breath. Instead, she seizes the opportunity to strike while my head is low, aiming her knee at my face. It's only my catlike reflexes that save me from a bleeding nose.

"You're good," I say around my mouthguard.

She rolls her eyes. "I've literally lived at a gym for eight years. What'd you expect?"

"Eight years?" I can hardly fathom it. She looks around the same age as me, perhaps a year or two older, so she must have only been a teenager when she left the country. Perhaps she found her way to the martial arts younger than I did. I was an aimless kid. The guy everyone liked, but who never really belonged. At least, not until I found MMA.

She jabs, and I slip the punch and haul her into a clinch. Her body presses against mine from thigh to chest, and it's the best sensation short of sex that I've ever experienced. The places where we touch are practically alight with the flames of attraction. With one leg, I try to sweep her to the floor, but she evades the movement and counters by rolling me over her hip. Her actions are less practiced than they have been until now, and I realize that's because she's not familiar with ground play. Throwing and wrestling are off the cards in muay thai.

A devilish grin steals across my face. Suddenly, there's nothing I want more than to get her on the floor, where she's at a disadvantage, just to see what she'll do. If I trap her in a hold, will she tap out? I doubt it. She's the type to be stubborn until she's blue in the face. As if she senses the direction of my thoughts, she shoves me away.

"You don't like getting up close and personal," I say.

She scowls. "Not true."

"Oh, so you want to get close to me?" I waggle my eyebrows, watching as her jaw tightens.

Instead of answering, she kicks the side of my body, then slams her padded shin into my thigh. Because I'm distracted, I'm too slow to check the kicks and if this fight were for real, she'd have scored a couple of clean points. She knows it, too. Her expression is smug, and I can't lie, her desire to prove she can beat the crap out of me is sexy as hell.

I launch into one of my favorite combos, curious how she'll react. She responds fluidly and within seconds, I find myself engaged in a dangerous dance. Sparring is one of my favorite pastimes, and she seems to feel the same because our bodies speak to each other as we move, and they're far more honest than our mouths. It's playful, but no longer tentative. We're learning each other's limitations and preferences. Our patterns and habits.

Yeah, I know. Sounds like sex.

Well, guess what? Sparring and sex have a lot in common. They're both weirdly intimate, and you have to trust a good sparring partner almost as much as you'd trust a sexual partner. After all, one false move and you eat a fist.

Seth approaches and starts barking instructions. They're directed at Harley so I tune them out, trying to figure out what throws her off her game. I'm unpredictable. That's my major tactic. I thrive on shocking people and then pressing my advantage, but Harley is unflappable in the face of my strategy, calmly returning blows and moving as though there's music only she can hear. For five rounds, we continue, with Seth drilling her during the breaks. *Try this. Do that. Don't let him get in your head.* I have to admit, I like the thought of being in her head. I want her thinking about me. Preferably wondering what's beneath my clothes. Not that she appears to be doing so, damn it all.

When we're done, I grab my drink bottle and towel, and wipe the sweat from my brow. Seth heads into his office, leaving me and Harley alone in the training area. A perfect opportunity.

Sidling over to her, I lower my voice and say, "Pretty sure you're my soul mate, Harls. Come zip-lining with me. It'll be fun."

She rolls her gorgeous hazel eyes. "You're being ridiculous."

"What?" I act shocked. "You don't want to be my soul mate?"

She flushes. Even though she's tanned—probably from training in the sun—her complexion is naturally fair and does nothing to hide the pinkness blossoming in her cheeks. It's fucking adorable. If I said that, she'd castrate me, but it's true. It also shows that she's not immune to the strange pull I'm feeling, she's just doing her best to pretend it isn't happening.

"You heard what Seth said," she grumbles, and looks away under the guise of reaching for her water.

"I did," I agree. "But as much as I respect him, my coach doesn't dictate my personal life, so as far as I'm concerned, that doesn't mean shit." Besides, Seth is my friend. He might be pissy if I date his sister at first, but once he sees I'm serious about her, it won't be a problem. "If you're not attracted to me—if you don't feel this tension between us—then come straight out and say it, and I'll leave you alone." Searching her eyes, I pray she doesn't pull the lever on the escape hatch I offered.

Her eyes narrow, but she shakes her head. "I can't do that."

Then she turns and stalks away, her ponytail swaying down the center of her back. I gulp. Round one to me. She's interested. I just need to work harder to woo her.

## Chapter Two

*HARLEY*

Seth's condo looks unlived in. Except for a small pile of laundry in the corner and a plate on the kitchen counter, there's not much indication that anyone spends their time here. But then, perhaps he doesn't. Mom is concerned he might be sleeping at the gym. She thinks having me around will give him a reason to come home. I haven't had the heart to tell her that I'm more likely to join him than nag him to return to the condo.

It has two bedrooms, an open plan living area, and one bathroom—which Seth is currently showering in. Fortunately, neither of us are fussy about our appearance so we're unlikely to fight over who gets to use the mirror in the mornings. Not that I intend on staying long. What man in his thirties wants his baby sister cramping his style? I'll be here until I get my feet beneath me, and then I'll find my own place.

It's evening now, the sun low in the sky, and I pull together a dinner of pad thai. There wasn't much in Seth's pantry so I had to make a trip to the supermarket, and I make sure to cook plenty because I know he'll want some as soon as he gets a whiff of it. The smell of the spices reminds me of the place I left behind, and a wave of homesickness crashes through me. I squeeze my eyes shut and wait for it to pass.

"You okay?"

My eyes fly open. Seth stands opposite me, his hair damp, wearing a freshly laundered t-shirt and jeans.

"Yeah, fine. Got onion juice in my eye."

"Uh-huh." The crinkle of his brow says he doesn't believe me. "Did you make me some?"

"Of course." I busy myself stirring dinner. "I'm taking advantage of your condo, so it's only fair."

He grins. "You gonna cook for me every night?"

I shrug. "I can do most, but I'm not sure how long I'll be hanging around. Depends if I find a place that's within my budget. Maybe if I get a roommate…" I trail off because I'm not a people person, but needs must and all that.

"Stay for as long as you like."

I glance at him, startled, and he chuckles.

"What? It's not as if I'm sneaking women home every night and shaking the building down with parties. There's no reason for you to hurry."

*Women.* It's strange to think of Seth with women because when we last saw each other, he was married and one hundred percent in love with his wife. The idea of him with anyone else feels wrong.

"I'm surprised you and Ashlin never patched things up," I admit, although I don't mention that I'm also disappointed. Ashlin is my friend. She's the kind of person who makes the world a better place simply by existing. I don't know what happened between her and Seth because neither will say, but any fool could tell they're perfect for each other.

His eyes darken, and his nostrils flare. Ever since he was a kid, he's gotten the same petulant expression when something displeases him, although at his current size, with his tattoos, it looks a little more menacing than when he was sixteen. He still doesn't frighten me though. He may only be my half-brother —each of us having a different father—but the "half" part never mattered to either of us.

"Let's not talk about her," he snaps. "In fact, let's make a deal. I won't ask about your corrupt ex-coach, and you won't mention Ashlin."

"Okay," I agree, because I don't need Seth digging into the situation with Thaklaew—a man who wasn't only my coach, but also my lover. I never mentioned that part to him because I was too ashamed to admit it. The fact that Thaklaew asked me to throw a fight was bad enough. The part that came after was worse. Even the memory hurts. His voice was slow and mean as he told me he'd been sleeping with other women who pleased him more than I did. Yeah, that was the icing on a crap cake, and if I have it my way, Seth and Mom will never find out. Even now, my gut churns at the memory.

"Why don't we talk strategy?" he suggests, as though sensing my discomfort. "You dish up, and I'll search for some videos of the other girls' fights on YouTube."

I nod. "Sounds good. Be there in a moment."

He goes into his room and emerges with a laptop, which he connects wirelessly to the TV. Meanwhile, I serve portions of pad thai into two bowls and carry them to his sofa, which is positioned behind a coffee table. I place one bowl in front of him and keep the other for myself.

"Seems like they taught you something other than

fighting in Thailand," he says as he takes his first taste. "This is better than any of the takeout places around here."

I laugh. "Of course it is. I didn't have anything to do except exercise and cook." And screw my coach. We kept that on the down low though, because it's hard enough getting respect as a female fighter without earning a reputation for being easy.

He brings up an image on the screen. "This is Katy Collins. Six pro fights. Three wins, three losses."

Except for her killer arms and shoulders, the girl on the screen looks like she'd be more at home in a cocktail bar than a cage. She has twinkling blue eyes, platinum blonde hair, and dimples. She looks nothing like the Thai warriors I've been facing off against for the past eight years.

"Don't be fooled by her smile. She has a mean right hook and two of her three wins were by knockout."

"Huh." Mentally, I slap myself. I should know better than to judge a book by its cover.

He brings up a photo of another woman and explains that she's Dutch, with a background in kick-boxing. As we eat, he introduces me to all seven of my potential opponents. I'll only be fighting three of them myself—presuming I make it to the final—but as for who I'll be facing, it's the luck of the draw. Amongst the possibilities is a black woman built like a tank, a girl with a shaved head and tattoos up her arms and neck, and a fan favorite who has been consistently doing well for herself over the past few years but still falling short of any major wins.

Once we've gone through the options, we discuss tactics. By the time I make it to bed, I'm exhausted and barely remember to brush my teeth before my head hits the pillow. The time difference is messing with me. Unfortunately, as soon as I close my eyes, a face flashes into my mind. Gorgeous brown eyes and a mischievous grin. Chiseled abs. Muscular calves.

*Devon Green.*

I try to shove him into a mental closet, but I can't turn off my curiosity. Sighing, I roll over and grab my phone from the nightstand. It seems I won't be sleeping until I've satisfied my need to know more about him. I enter his name into Google and get thousands of hits—most of them are actually him, even though the name is relatively common. Scrolling through images, I see shots from his fights and weigh-ins, and a bunch of him at parties, dressed nicely with a different girl hanging off his arm each time. His eyes seem to twinkle, but my heart takes a dive.

He's a player. Of course he is. He's too good-looking not to be, and while he was definitely flirting with me at the gym, I should know better than to think there's something special about me. He probably flirts with every girl he meets.

Disgusted with myself, I click onto a YouTube video of him fighting a blond guy the caption identifies as Karson Hayes, hating how relieved I am not to have to see him with other women anymore. It's crazy and ridiculous, but my mind keeps telling me that him being with them is wrong. The date on the video shows the fight was a couple years ago, but even then, Devon was good. His style is unpredictable. A little strange, but effective.

On the screen, Karson's foot whips up and strikes the side of Devon's head, and he drops like a rock. I wince. *Eesh.* At least, he *was* effective until that happened. The referee counts to eight, then calls an end to the fight. I shut my phone down and place it back on the nightstand, trying to erase Devon—and the memory of how electric it felt to spar with him—from my mind.

Then I dream of him.

*Fuck.*

---

DEVON

"Yoohoo! Anyone home?" I call as I enter Jase's house—or should I say mansion? "The door is unlocked. I'll just make myself at home."

I settle on the sofa, which is huge and comfortable. Jase is accustomed to me and Gabe crashing his place unexpectedly. The three of us have been training together at Crown MMA Gym for years now, and they're the closest thing I have to brothers. I know they feel the same, even if they don't come out and say it. There's a noise somewhere in the private quarters, and I lean back, stretching my legs out in front of me.

"Fuck off!" Jase yells from the direction of his bedroom.

I grin. He's probably getting it on with Lena, his girlfriend. Those two can't keep their hands off each other. "It's cool, bro. I'll wait. I'm sure it won't be long."

He swears again, and a few moments later, he and Lena emerge, each righting their clothing. Lena's face is the color of her hair—red.

"Hi Devon," she says, grinning in a way that says she knows I know what they've been up to, and she doesn't care. That's what I love about Lena. She's got fire. Not as much as Harley, though.

"You didn't have to hurry on my account."

She rolls her eyes. "Tell that to Jase. Apparently, you're quite the distraction."

I nod. "I hear that all the time."

Jase groans as he tugs his t-shirt over his head, covering up the tattoos across his chest and shoulders. "Why, bro? Why couldn't you let me have one night of peace?"

"Because." I pause for dramatic effect. "I'm in love."

His eyes bug out of his head, then he snorts. "With who?"

Lena drops onto the sofa beside me and leans forward like an eager kid. "Tell us everything."

"Harley Isles," I declare, watching the shock cross their faces. "I met her this morning and I can already tell that she's the woman for me. No fucking doubt about it."

Jase buries his face in his hands. "Harley? Please say you're joking."

"I'm as serious as I've ever been." On second thought, I add, "More serious." Because if we're being honest, seriousness is not a strength of mine.

"Who's Harley?" Lena asks, looking from me to Jase and back again.

"She's Seth's baby sister." Jase flops into an armchair and shakes his head. "Leave her alone, Dev. You've just got a crush because you know Seth would string you up if you even looked at her sideways."

"Not true," I counter. "Have you met her? If you had, it wouldn't seem so unbelievable. She's gorgeous, and a total badass."

"I haven't met her," he admits, running a hand through the ends of his hair. "But I know you, and it's probably just a crush. Promise me you won't act on it, because you'll regret it within a week if you do. Trust me. I'm not trying to be a dick. I'm looking out for you."

I frown. I know he means well, but I'd hoped he might be happy for me. The last loner of our three-some finally meeting someone who could take him down a peg.

"I can't promise that. I told you, I think she's the one." Something aches in my chest and I rub it. The thought of leaving her alone feels wrong all the way down to my bones. "I won't do anything to make Seth lose his shit though."

Fortunately, Lena seems to read my expression because she smiles softly and tucks her hair behind an ear. "Tell me about her."

"That's more like it." I force myself to grin. "There's the enthusiasm I wanted to see. Hmm, where should I start?"

"What does she do?"

Jase grunts. "I can't believe you're indulging him."

She ignores the cranky fucker. "Go on."

"From what I understand, she's been a professional muay thai fighter in Thailand for the past eight years, but she's just moved here and Seth is debuting her as his first female pro fighter."

"Oh, wow." Her eyes light up with curiosity. "I have so many questions. How old is she? Because I would have thought, being Seth's sister, that she was on the high end of the age scale for an athlete."

I shrug. "Not sure. Maybe mid-twenties. Much younger than him, anyway. Momma Isles might have had an oopsies baby."

"She's twenty-six," Jase mutters, eyeing us as though he resents us for making him a part of this conversation.

"There you go. Only a year older than me, and

she's hot as hell." I grab my phone from my pocket and pull up a photo of her beside a Thai guy who might be her coach that I found online. In it, she's wearing gloves, a sports bra, and a crooked smile, her hair slicked back against her forehead and her eyes gleaming with triumph.

Lena cocks her head and appraises her. "I have to say, she's not who I saw you ending up with." I start to scowl, but then she adds, "She's much better."

*Damn right, she is.*

"Who did you see me with?" I ask, unable to resist.

She grins. "A busty babe who'd be content to hang off your every word and inflate your massive ego."

I should be insulted by that, but in the moment, I don't give a shit.

"She's a babe, that's for sure." Studying the photo more carefully, I notice the way the man's hand rests possessively on her shoulder, and I don't like it. A sense of wrongness blares in my head. Switching the screen off, I decide not to look at it anymore. I'll find a better picture.

"Is she as smitten with you as you are with her?" Lena asks.

Jase scoffs, and we both glance at him. "I may not have met her, but I doubt Harley Isles is the type to be smitten."

"I'll bring her around." Maybe she was hesitant about me, but we were vibing. That zing of awareness between us can't be faked, and she didn't take the opportunity to shoot me down when I handed it to her on a silver platter. "She definitely felt something."

"Good for you," Lena says.

"Thank you, beautiful." I wink at her, and Jase glares. He knows I'm teasing though. If he didn't, I'd have found myself in a choke hold within seconds. "I was hoping Jase might be able to fill in some of the blanks about her."

He crosses his arms over his chest, flexing his muscles, and Lena licks her lips. What I wouldn't give for a woman to look at me that way. "Like what?"

"Anything you got, man. I didn't even know she existed until you mentioned her a few days ago. I need details."

"God." He rubs his eyelids. "Couldn't you have gone to Gabe?"

"Nah, I thought about it, but he's with a girl he's known his whole life. You had to win Lena over from scratch, so you'll give better advice."

"I hate how logical that is. Fine." He huffs. "I don't actually know a heap about her. She moved to Thailand at eighteen and settled at a gym. I never heard Seth mention a boyfriend or serious relationship, but he's pretty tight-lipped, so who the hell knows whether that means anything."

"Perhaps she's a career woman," Lena suggests, giving me a slightly sympathetic look that says more than her words do. "Not interested in relationships."

"Or maybe she just didn't tell her hot-tempered big brother, who's built like a freight train and has a wall full of awards for kicking ass, about her sex life." If I were her, I'd be keeping Seth far, far away from any man I intended to see more than once. I'd do nearly anything for the guy, but he's scary as hell at times.

"Maybe," Lena allows.

"How many fights has she had?" I ask Jase. "I couldn't find an official record online."

"I don't know." He scratches his jaw. "Maybe seventy or eighty."

I gape. "Holy shit. Are you having me on?"

Seventy or eighty fights is fucking intense. I've had

six professional fights and maybe ten or fifteen amateurs. But seventy? That's a whole other league. My respect for her skyrockets.

"Nope." He shakes his head. "They don't pay fighters much in Thailand, so they tend to fight every month or so, although the women generally get fewer than the men because the pool of competitors is smaller."

"That's insane. But kinda awesome." I ponder the idea. I love fighting. Maybe I should move to Thailand. That said, I'd hate to lose the freedom of being able to grapple as well as strike. Jiu-jitsu is a ton of fun. "So, next to her, I'm an eenie weenie baby fighter."

"Basically," he agrees. "As long as she can get her ground work up to scratch, those girls she's been matched against won't stand a chance."

"Huh." Something occurs to me. "She's had more fights than Seth."

"Yeah, but that doesn't mean anything in terms of coaching." This comes from Lena. "The most prolific athletes don't necessarily make the best coaches. Seth's secret is tough love and loyalty." She gives me a meaningful look. "So don't screw it up. I'm all for you finding love, but don't stab him in the back."

"I won't." While I may not always follow the rules, I'm an open person. It's not in my nature to betray anyone. "Do you know what she likes to do other than muay thai?"

"Nah. Sorry, bro, I never paid much attention."

"Damn it. I need an inside source on Harley Isles." I glance at Lena. "I don't suppose you'd be willing to go undercover as a double agent and figure out what makes her tick?"

She rolls her eyes. "I'm not doing your dirty work for you."

My phone vibrates and I check the screen, deleting the message as soon as I see it's from one of the girls I met at Gabe's fight yesterday. Maybe it makes me a douche, but I can hardly remember her face. My mind is full of Harley, and I have no interest in a substitute.

"Whoa, this just got serious," Jase says. "Did you just delete an invitation to hook up?"

"Yeah." It's no big deal. From now on, I have no room in my bed for any woman other than Harley.

# Chapter Three

*HARLEY*

On Monday morning, Crown MMA Gym is bustling. By the time I rock up, having slept longer than I'd have liked, there are half a dozen people hitting bags, being taken through pads, or using the weights in the corner. I spot Devon immediately, working with a big Samoan man who has tattoos everywhere. My brother is in the cage with a lean white guy who's perhaps twenty or so, and whose ash blond hair is tied back in a ponytail, much the same as mine.

I kick my shoes off, stuff my bag in a locker, and grab a skipping rope. Thirty minutes pass as I observe the action around me, a little surprised that no one has approached. I expected questions. Curiosity. But except for a few glances, none of the men seem interested in talking to me. Even Devon hasn't come anywhere near me, although he's met my eyes once or twice and smirked in a way that makes me think he knows what I dreamed about last night. But he can't, right? It's all in my head.

When I finish, I hang up the rope and stretch. I'm on my back, working on my hamstrings when a face appears above me. Slate gray eyes, a stubbly jaw, and cheekbones sharp enough to cut. I recognize him immediately. Jase Rawlins, one of the first fighters Seth worked with, who's been with him for years. I don't know whether Jase is aware or not, but Seth considers him a younger brother. Jase offers a hand, and I take it and leap to my feet.

"Nice to finally meet you," I say, smiling. "I hear you're going to teach me how to grapple."

"Sure am." His lips curl in a slow, cocky grin that probably drives women crazy—although I believe he's off the market these days. I'm sure teenage girls with crushes are crying into their pillows all over the country. "You'll be unbeatable by the time I'm done with you."

"Perfect. I'm not sure how much Seth's told you, but I need to be able to win three fights in one night, and I've got two months to do it."

He nods. "The eliminator. He mentioned it to me. For what it's worth, I think it's incredible what you're doing."

Something warms inside me. I love the respect I see in his expression. It's not always something I come by easily, and it's nice to know that I have someone other than Seth onside.

"Thanks." I roll my shoulders, loosening them up. "I was going to do a few rounds on bags. Did you just come over to say hi, or are we grappling now?"

"We'll do it now." He glances at the electronic timer that's counting down on the wall. "Start of the next round. I'll talk you through some basic moves and give you a chance to practice. Then, afterward, we'll roll, so you can try them when you're under pressure."

"Sounds good." I drink from my bottle, mop sweat off my face and neck, and wrap my hands so I'm ready to go when the timer beeps.

Over the next five rounds, Jase demonstrates an armbar and several maneuvers with the word "choke" in their names. It's a somewhat unpleasant experience. Striking and taking hits is one thing, but I'm not used to trying to fight when there's no blood or air getting to my brain. It adds a whole new aspect to the game. Not to mention I'm genuinely afraid he might break my arm. But I'm a trooper and I didn't give up my life in Thailand just to fail. I'm determined to learn each and every thing he shows me.

When we're freestyling, and I tap out for the third time in a row and flop back against the mat, gasping for breath, I have to admit to being out of my depth. The thing I like about Jase, though, is that he doesn't treat me differently than anyone else. He doesn't go easy on me, or hold back his full strength for fear of hurting me. He goes just as hard as he would with a man, and even though I'm struggling, I know I'll be better for it in the long run.

"Yo, Dev!" he calls across the room as he lets me catch my breath. "You sub in. I want to coach her from the outside. See where she's going wrong."

Closing my eyes, I stifle a groan. *Great. Just great.* As if I'm not having a hard enough time without introducing Devon and his sexy lips to the equation.

*Treat him like any other sparring buddy,* I tell myself. *Because that's all he is. That's all he can be.*

I roll to my feet, and find him far closer than I'd thought, almost chest to chest with me. My nipples want to poke holes in my sports bra to get to him.

"Harley." He dips his head in acknowledgment, and there's a gleam in his eye that I shouldn't like but do. Jase clears his throat, and gives Devon a look with a little censure in it. What's that about?

"Rein in the crazy," Jase tells him. "She's just learning, so we're working through the basics. She doesn't need you pulling any of your weird-ass moves."

"Got it, boss." He salutes, and I have to laugh. He's so irreverent, and any female with eyes would find his cheeky smirk appealing.

"Harley"—Jase turns to me—"don't overcomplicate things. Your number one focus at the moment should be taking advantage of any opportunity you see to get him into a hold, but otherwise, get on top or upright as soon as possible, since that's where your strengths are."

"Okay." I lower myself to the floor, and Devon faces me. Awareness flutters through me and the nerves in my abdomen come to life. It's ridiculous, but I'd swear I can sense the heat of him near me, and that both of our pulse rates have doubled. The space between our bodies is charged, and his pupils dilate, his eyes nearly black. I can't bring myself to look away.

What's wrong with me? I've never been turned on during training before. Not even when I was banging my coach. There's no way the slightest brush of Thaklaew's skin against mine would have had me on the verge of shivering.

The timer sounds, and we launch into action. Our bodies move with the grace of two people who are hyperalert to the barest change or movement in the other. Somehow, the distraction of his sleek muscles gliding over mine takes the edge off my nerves and my actions are much smoother than they were with Jase. He tries to shift me into an armbar, but I extricate myself before he has me stuck, then I tuck his head

26

into a choke hold and he slips fluidly out of it before I can lock him in.

We're rolling on the floor, our movements more of a dance than a battle for dominance. I take charge temporarily, then he shifts the balance of power. Somewhere in the back of my mind, I can hear Jase issuing instructions, but I'm operating on instinct more than anything else. The round ends, and I pin Devon to the floor, staring down at him. There's an animal expression written across his features that I'm certain must be echoed in mine. He wants me, and he can't hide it.

Something long and hard pulses between my legs, and my eyes widen. Now he *definitely* can't hide it. He looks as stunned as I am, but neither of us move. He's stuck where he is unless he wants someone to know the condition he's in, and I'm so shocked it doesn't even occur to me to get off him. This has never happened before. When his expression becomes pleading, it makes me think it's a new situation for him, too.

"Think unsexy thoughts," I hiss. "I can't cover for you forever."

His gaze rakes up and down my body and he gives me a helpless look. "You're kinda making that hard."

I snort. The situation isn't the only thing that's hard, and I have the strangest urge to rub myself all over him.

"What the hell are you guys up to?" Jase asks, right on cue, putting an end to my wayward thoughts.

"Devon is explaining the half guard to me," I say, even though we're clearly in the wrong position for that.

"He'd better speed it up, or people are going to get uncomfortable." Jase's tone indicates that he's already uncomfortable.

Devon gives me a slight nod, and I climb off him. I

guess hearing his friend's voice is enough to ruin the mood.

"Thanks," he murmurs, and then takes off toward the bathroom.

---

*DEVON*

It should be illegal for anyone to be this turned on during training. Shame oppresses all other emotions as I scuttle off to the bathroom like a kid who's peed their pants, then shut myself in a cubicle.

It was the fire in her eyes that did it, and the way it felt to have her toned legs wrapped around me. Am I going to spring a boner every time I spar with her? Because that's both awfully inconvenient and fucking embarrassing. The only reason I'm not the laughing-stock of every guy here—and Seth's personal whipping boy—is because she took pity on me and helped me hide my reaction to her. If she'd been repulsed and made a scene, I'd never be taken seriously again. Thank fuck she's a decent person who isn't horrified by random erections. In fact, for a moment, it seemed like she was as caught up in the attraction as I was, with a flush on her cheeks that had nothing to do with exertion, and a softness to her body that was all about man-woman chemistry.

"Fuck," I mutter, picturing her blushing that same way as I slide inside her. Just like that, my dick is hard again. Squeezing my eyes shut, I reach into my shorts to adjust it, but the contact sends a bolt of heat shooting down my spine and I groan and wrap my fist around it.

*I can't jerk off in the gym bathroom, can I?*

It's a terrible, disrespectful idea, but I also don't see

how I can return to training in my current state, so I give my cock a lone tug and take my bottom lip between my teeth to keep from making a sound. Shit, I'm close to coming already. With a sigh—and praying like hell that no one walks in—I shove my shorts all the way down, cup my balls in one hand and start stroking. It's fast, furious, and with no finesse at all, but at this point, it's a practicality and nothing more. I just need to deal with the problem so I can get back out there.

I return to the mental image of Harley's face as I drive into her. In my mind, it's not my hand I'm pumping into, it's her pussy, and it's slippery and ready for me. My imaginary Harley plays with her nipples, which are perfect pink buds, and then I'm coming, my thighs trembling as I empty myself. Resting my forehead against the wall, I wait for my heart to stop jackhammering. When it's calmed, I clean up my mess, pull my shorts back up, and wash my hands. For good measure, I splash cold water on my face.

As I step back into the training area, Jase glances over and narrows his eyes, but he doesn't approach. He probably suspects what I've been doing but doesn't want to ask because he doesn't want to think about it. Can't say I blame him. The new guy, Jimmy, has taken over sparring with Harley, and jealously strums at the strings of my heart. I don't want any other man that close to her, not unless he's neutered or already off the market. But given her profession, I guess I'd better get used to it.

For the next half hour, I take my frustration out on the heavy bags, and once I've recovered enough to be less ashamed of myself, I wait for a break between rounds and approach her. She's moved on from grappling and is doing squats. I force myself not to look at her firm, rounded ass because that way lies trouble.

"Thank you for covering for me."

"Don't mention it."

"Want to come go-karting with me after training?" I ask. It's the first activity that pops to mind, and I get the impression it's the sort of thing she'd enjoy. "My treat, as an apology."

"No, thanks." She doesn't even pause in her squatting to shoot me down.

I clutch my hand to my heart and affect a wounded expression. "I swear, I have the best of intentions."

She raises a brow, and her eyes dip to my crotch. "Uh-huh."

Okay, so there's not much I can say to that.

"Is it me, or the go-karting?" I ask.

"A bit of both."

I nod. I can respect that. She needs more time to adjust to the idea of us, but she's definitely attracted to me. I can tell by the way her gaze lingers on my body. Still, I need her to say it, otherwise I feel like a persistent creep.

"You're not uninterested in me though?"

She hesitates, then inclines her head. "I guess you could say that."

"Good." I can work with that. If she's reluctant, or has some concerns, I can figure out a way to address those. I wink, and open my mouth to say something flirty, but then spot Seth watching us out of the corner of my eye, and instead I jerk my chin at her the way I might with one of the guys and stride away.

Did I leave her wanting more?

I sure as hell hope so.

## Chapter Four

*HARLEY*

For the rest of the week, I find Devon every time I turn around. Smiling at me, winking at me, giving me that cocksure look that says he knows exactly what to do with a woman when her body responds to him the way mine does. My hormones are out of whack, my nerves constantly on edge. The man is intruding on my peace of mind.

What's worse is the way I'm coming to admire him. He may be a loose cannon, but he treats everyone well and he's passionate about MMA. In fact, he might be the only person who trains as long and hard as I do. The difference is that he probably blows off steam with parties and women in the evenings whereas I crash on the couch with Seth to watch TV or meditate in my room.

His flirtatiousness is growing on me too, and no matter how hard I try, I can't erase the memory of his hard dick beneath me. By the time Friday comes, I'm starting to wonder if it wouldn't be the worst thing to go to bed with him once or twice. My body is tired of being in a constant state of arousal, and it's not as if I haven't had casual sex before. Besides, any loyalty I may have felt toward Thaklaew is gone.

When I enter the gym after returning from a run, I'm immediately greeted by one of his perusals that's so heated I may as well be naked. He doesn't even have to touch me, and I want to strip off all his clothes and ride him like a wild mustang. Based on the way his lips curl slowly, he's aware of his effect on me. Would it really hurt so much to be with him once and get it out of my system? It's not as if he'd want anything more than that. Men like him get bored with women like me. Maybe I could find out what he's capable of, just to satisfy my curiosity.

*No. Bad Harley. Sleeping with someone from your gym is part of what got you into this mess.*

Devon isn't Thaklaew though, and it wouldn't be a relationship, just a quick fuck. I don't have any feelings for him, other than professional admiration. He's hot, that's all. That body... My gaze dips to his strong thighs, and I swallow. *Very* hot.

"Harley, you're with me," Seth barks across the gym, holding up a couple of Thai pads. Shaking away thoughts of Devon, I slip on a pair of gloves and join him. He takes me through a few rounds, issuing instructions while I punch, kick, knee, elbow, slip, and weave. It's while I'm practicing my low kicks that I sense a change in the atmosphere and glance toward the entrance. A pretty black woman with her hair tied back is hovering just inside the door, looking around.

"Who's that?" I ask Seth as I aim a straight right at the pad in his hand.

"Sydney. Gabe's girl."

"Hey, Syd." I hear Devon's voice behind me, deep

and welcoming. "You're looking particularly beautiful today. Is there a special occasion I don't know about?"

My heart sinks and I don't hear her reply. He's flirting with her. Of course he is. I've already ascertained that he's a flirt. He's not truly interested in her, but perhaps that means he's not truly interested in me either, and I've been silly to take his winks and smiles to heart. Maybe he's just messing with me the same way he is with Sydney—because it's in his nature and he enjoys it.

I'm a fool.

Setting my jaw, I make up my mind to pay him no heed in future.

"Left hook," Seth calls, and I smash my fist into the pad with all the power and aggression I can muster. Unfortunately, it doesn't make me feel any better.

Five minutes later, I'm doing crunches in the corner when I hear a quiet voice saying my name.

"Harley?"

Pausing, I roll into a seated position and look up to see Sydney standing over me. Up close, I can see she has deep brown eyes, flawless skin, and a kind smile.

"I'm Sydney. It's nice to meet you."

"You too," I say, getting up and thrusting my hand out before realizing it's sweaty as hell and she probably doesn't want to touch me. She takes it anyway. "You're dating Gabe?"

"Yeah." She smiles, and tucks her hair behind her ear. "It's very new, but we've been best friends basically since first grade."

My heart squeezes at the way her eyes soften. It's clear she's in love, and for some reason, envy grips me for a few seconds before I manage to dismiss it. I've never wanted a perfect romance before, so I don't know why her obvious giddiness gets to me.

"That's pretty cool," I reply, wishing I had something better to offer.

"Yeah." She tilts her head. "I know all of the guys here, and you're in good hands."

"Thanks." I study her, wondering if there's a reason she came over other than to introduce herself. She seems to have something on her mind.

"Did you know one of the newbies has a fight tomorrow night?" she asks. "Jase and Seth will both be there to corner him. Gabe, too. He's taking a break from training, but he'll still be helping out with things like this from time to time."

I nod. Seth has mentioned the event. Apparently he has some concerns about whether the fighter is up to the task, but not because of any lack of training, just that his attitude is a bit off.

"Anyway, Lena—that's Jase's girlfriend—and I are getting together while they're at the fight, and we'd love for you to join us."

"Really?" I hadn't expected that, and I'm not sure how to respond. I haven't had female friends I could just hang out with in over eight years. The only ones I've kept up relationships with trained with me at the gym, and we lived muay thai. Then there's Ashlin, but considering we've been in different countries, it's not as if we've had the chance to spend time together.

"Of course." She smiles, and it hits me that she looks truly happy. Not many people can claim that. "Being around all this testosterone is a lot of work. You need some girl time to balance it out."

At this, I can't help but smile. She does have a point. Sometimes I get so caught up in all the manly energy floating around that I find myself trying to compete with it.

"Okay, then. I'd like that. Thanks so much for inviting me."

"Great!" She beams. "We'll be at Lena's place. She lives with Jase. I don't know the address off the top of my head, but Seth will have it, and if not, just get my number from him and I can find out for you. I'll see you around six?"

"Perfect."

She gives me a little wave. "Can't wait. I'll let you get back to business. You must have to train insanely hard to keep up with all these men."

"Bye, nice to meet you." I return to crunches, but my mind is whirling. Eight years is a long time to forget how to interact with women who aren't part of the martial arts community. Although, I guess in a way, Sydney and Lena are part of that community. The thought comforts me somewhat. But still, will I have anything in common with them? Or will it be one of those nights where I sit there, unsure of what to say? I hope it's the former. I could really use some friends in my life.

---

*DEVON*

Damn it. I was so close to winning Harley over, I could practically taste her sassy lips on my own. She's been laughing at my jokes—even if she glares afterward to make it clear she doesn't mean to—and nearly every time I seek her out, I find her already watching me. But ever since Sydney visited, she's gone cold, and I'm not sure why. I don't know what's going on in her head, but it's nothing good. At least, not where I'm concerned.

Unfortunately, I don't know how to fix it. I glance

over at her as she attacks a kick-bag with vigor, her back pointedly turned toward me. Her form is fucking amazing, because of course it is. She's a warrior princess. The bell sounds, and she stops kicking, turning to grab her water bottle. Her eyes catch on mine and the air between us seems to cool ten degrees. I offer a smile. She scowls in response.

"Dev."

I glance over at Jase, who's standing behind me, presumably just having witnessed the nonverbal rejection. I decide not to let it bother me. I knew Harley wouldn't be easy to win over, and it's only been a week.

"Haven't heard about any of your conquests lately," he says, walking closer and dropping his voice. "Is that because of Harley?"

I shrug. "Yeah, I told you, I'm not interested in anyone other than her."

Gabe, who's dropped by to run over the plan for tomorrow evening, stops abruptly beside us. "What?"

I wince. That's right. I'd forgotten he wasn't there when I declared my feelings.

"Shh," I hiss, because the last thing I need is for her to know we're talking about her. Judging by the looks coming my way, she's annoyed enough without being the subject of gossip.

Gabe raises a brow. "You're the one who mentioned it."

"Actually, Jase is," I point out. "But yeah, I'm into her, and I'm pretty sure she's into me. She just doesn't know what to do about it."

Gabe narrows his eyes. "She's Seth's sister."

"I know," I mutter, "and it's damned inconvenient."

"Against the rules, too," Jase reminds me.

"Yeah, yeah." Do they have to gang up on me? I

36

know that pursuing her isn't the most noble thing to do, but I also want to make sure there's something between us before announcing to Seth that I want to court his sister, or some old-fashioned shit like that.

"Are you sure that isn't why you're interested in her?" Gabe asks. "The allure of the forbidden?"

Snorting with laughter, I cover my mouth. "Bro, did you just say 'allure'?"

He rubs a hand on the back of his neck, cheeks flushing. "Sydney's rubbing off on me."

I shake my head, not even wanting to think about all the "rubbing" he and Sydney do. She's a great girl, and I knew her for years before they hooked up, so I do not want to think about all the filthy things they probably do to each other.

"That's not what it is. I like her, man. Really like her." So much that the sight of her delivering the world's most perfect roundhouse kick has fucking flutters erupting in my belly. *Flutters.*

"You hardly know her."

I grasp at the fraying ends of my temper. They're treating me like a naughty child, and they may not mean to, but it's bothering me. They're supposed to know me better than anyone else. What does it say about me that they think I only want her because I can't have her?

"I know enough."

Jase hums in thought. "She's clearly not interested. Maybe you should just let this go and pick up a woman at the fights tomorrow? I'm sure there are plenty who'll want to go home with 'Dangerous' Devon Green."

"No." Honestly, I can't believe he'd suggest such a thing. "Would you have done that when the only woman you wanted was Lena?"

"No," he admits.

"Then don't try to pressure me into it. I don't care whether you understand or not, but Harley and I have a connection, and I'm not going to rush it, and I'm not going to do anything to mess it up."

He claps me on the shoulder. "Good for you, bro. Just be careful."

"And don't screw over Seth," Gabe adds.

"I won't." I'm not the kind of guy to betray his friends for a girl... am I?

# Chapter Five

*HARLEY*

When Seth and several of the guys leave the gym to head to fights on Saturday, the only person I know who's left after they're gone is Devon. There are a couple of other men sparring and lifting weights, but I haven't said more than "hi" to them since I moved here.

"Harley, want to spar?"

I spin to face Devon, who's voiced the question. He's wearing gloves and has a towel slung around his neck. He's also not wearing a shirt, so his sexy chest is on display. My mouth waters, and I'm struck by the insane urge to lick the groove down the center of his six-pack.

*Hello, crazy town. Paging Harley. Come back to earth.*

"Uh, yeah, sounds good. But actually, I need to work on grappling rather than striking, so how about we roll?"

He flashes his signature mischievous grin, and heat pools low in my stomach. Why did I suggest that? What was I thinking? I shouldn't be inviting him to rub that bare, muscled body all over me. But then, grappling *is* my weak spot and I *do* need to work on it. I wait for him to drop to the ground first, because I'm certainly not going to be the one to do it. He lowers himself to his knees and I rush to follow suit because otherwise I'll start having fantasies about him leaning in and burying his face in my pussy, and that shit can't happen.

"Eager to get on top of me, huh?" he quips, and a flush heats my cheeks because he's hit closer to the truth than he probably realizes. "All right, show me what you've got."

I go for the attack, hoping that the sooner my body falls into the familiar pattern of sparring, the faster all of my crazy hormones will calm down. I pin him, and throw some gentle punches at his face to pressure him to make a move.

"So, why are you here and not at the fight?" I ask.

"Seth didn't want me psyching out the new kid, so I'll be heading over to help out once they've got him in a good headspace." He speaks from behind arms that are forming a shield.

"Do you do like psyching people out?"

"Maybe a little," he admits. "It's fun."

Fast as a flash, he bucks his hips and rolls into action, dislodging me. Out of habit, I get to my feet, but he wraps his arms around me and brings me back to the floor. I test some of the maneuvers Jase taught me, but in the end, Devon gets me on my back, open and vulnerable. His lower body presses into mine, and a wave of heat crashes through me. Suddenly, I want nothing more than for him to close the distance between our mouths.

His nostrils flare, and his eyes darken impossibly, as though he can read my thoughts. He leans forward, resting his weight on his forearms, my head caged between them. Slowly, his lips descend toward me. Every part of me craves the kiss, from the tips of my curled toes, to my peaked nipples, to my tingling lips. His breath tickles my skin like a caress, and something inside me freaks the fuck out.

I can't kiss Devon Green on the floor of my brother's gym.

I can't kiss him, full stop.

He's the kind of guy who'll break my heart, and I've been hurt enough for one year. With moves I never even knew I possessed, I flip us, smacking him into the ground. His eyes widen in shock, and he gasps as the sudden impact winds him.

Leaping to my feet, I back away, hand to my mouth. "Oh, my God. I'm so sorry. I didn't mean to do that."

To my complete and utter astonishment, he bursts out laughing, and stares up at me, shaking his head in amusement. "That was hot as hell." He raises a gloved hand, and I grab it and yank him to his feet. "You got me." He bumps my fist with his. "Nice one, Isles."

"It wasn't intentional," I mutter.

"Even better." He winks. "If that's what you can do by mistake, just imagine what you'll do to those girls when you're trying."

The thought brightens my mood. I hope he's right. I'm glad he's being nice about this. A lot of men would feel emasculated or led on.

"So," he continues, rubbing circles on his chest. "This is the part where I ask you out again, yeah?"

I sigh. "If it was, I'd have to turn you down." Strangely, I find myself regretting that fact, and not just because my body is still wired with attraction to him. He actually seems like a nice guy, but officially off-limits, and not the right match for me anyway.

"Damn." His lips quirk, but he doesn't seem upset at all. "Have you decided whether you want me to back off and stop flirting with you?"

My breath quickens. Why does he have to keep asking that and putting the responsibility on me to reject him? Why can't he be like any other douchey guy who'd ignore what I want and flirt anyway? Because while I can't date him, I enjoy exchanging hot looks across the gym floor and I don't want it to end.

"No, I haven't," I say, something fizzing in my chest. "I need more time to think about it."

"Okay, then." He grins crookedly. "Can I ask what's holding you back?"

I drag a hand down my face and battle to pull myself together. Dare I be honest with him? I moisten my lips. "The thing is, I've recently gone through something that makes it hard for me to trust people, and I'm not denying that I'm attracted to you, but you seem like a good-time guy and that's not what I'm looking for."

He cocks his head, the humor fleeing his expression, and his eyes become uncharacteristically serious. "I could be more than a good-time guy for you, Harley."

A lick of heat runs down my spine. His gaze is so intense. So honest. But from what I've seen of him, I'm not sure whether to believe him. The fact is, I hardly know Devon. I knew Thaklaew much better, and I still didn't see his betrayal coming. Why should I think I'm any better at reading this guy?

"Think on it." He touches his glove to mine. "Ready for round two?"

Before heading to the stadium to watch the fights, I drop by my parents' place for a visit. Jamal and Rochelle Green live in a solidly middle class neighborhood, surrounded by houses that are nice but nothing fancy, and they're likely to stay there until the day they die. Even if I make it big in MMA and start raking in the amount of money that Gabe and Jase do from sponsorships, I doubt they'll want to move. They fit here, and that's important to them. I, on the other hand, never fit. I used to try to squeeze myself into their templated idea of who I should be, but eventually I gave up, and so did they. Perhaps they decided to blame our differences on the fact I'm not biologically theirs, but who knows? All I can say is our relationship has improved a hell of a lot since we accepted that we're not built of the same stuff.

I knock on the door and wait for Mom to open it. She's a short lady with rich, dark skin, a pixie cut, and a no-nonsense tone.

"Well, hello. Fancy seeing you." She steps aside. "Come in." She eyes the t-shirt I'm wearing, which has the logo for the gym printed on the front. "Are you on your way somewhere?"

"One of our guys has his first professional fight tonight," I tell her. "Gotta show my support and be there to ice his shins if they need it."

She shakes her head. "When are you going to choose a safer, more stable career? You've been trying this MMA thing for a while now. Surely it's time to move on."

She starts up the hall, leading the way to the living area, and I follow. This is a common conversation for us. Try as they might, she and Dad just can't understand my choices or my dreams. They seem to believe that MMA is a phase I'm going to grow out of, but I'm persistent as hell, and while I'm not a household name yet, all it will take is a couple of big opportunities to break through the barrier to fame.

"MMA is it for me. Sorry, Mom."

She shakes her head, and gestures for me to take a seat at the dining table with my dad while she puts the kettle on. "Tea? Coffee?"

"Coffee, please." I smile at Dad. "Hey, Pops. How you doing?"

He sets down his book—a biography, by the looks of it—and returns my smile. "Good to see you, son." Like Mom, his gaze drops to my shirt. "Still repping the gym, I see."

I wince at his use of the word "repping". There are some things people over fifty just shouldn't say. "That's right. Life's too short not to do something you love."

Although neither of them can fathom that. Dad is a dentist, and Mom is a church secretary. She's constantly praying for my eternal soul.

His lips press together. "I'll never understand why you love being punched in the face and inflicting pain on others."

Gritting my teeth, I try not to say anything I'll regret. "Maybe if you came to one of my bouts and watched me, you'd get it."

Mom pours two coffees and a tea and places them on a tray. "I don't need to watch my baby get hurt." She carries the tray to the table and distributes the drinks. "Why must you keep tempting fate? You've survived—"

"A car wreck, a fall from the roof, and a run-in with a burglar," I interrupt, knowing exactly what's

<44>44</44>

coming. This is a common refrain from her. The trouble is, she and I view it differently. "I survived all of those things because it wasn't my time to go. When it's my time, it's my time, regardless of how often I get into the cage."

Her lips wobble, and her eyes gloss over. I mentally kick myself, feeling like an asshole. I know she's genuinely worried, but I'm never going to give up my passion just to pacify her. She sips her tea and we sit in silence for a long moment.

Finally, she asks, "Have you met a nice girl to settle down with?"

Despite myself, I chuckle. This is our other regular discussion, and she's used to me shutting it down quickly. I'm about to shock the hell out of her.

"As a matter of fact, I have."

She gasps, then claps a hand to her mouth before she can spray tea all over the table. "Dev!" she chokes as she swallows. "Couldn't you have had the good grace to wait until I didn't have a mouthful of liquid to drop that bombshell on us?"

I shrug, feeling all kinds of gleeful. I'm not one of those guys who needs his mommy's approval but damned if it isn't nice to have it from time to time. "You asked."

"I expected you to say the same thing you always do."

"Career before relationships," Dad intones, mimicking me.

A grin spreads over my face. "Well, it turns out that I don't have to choose."

Mom's brow furrows. "What do you mean?"

"The girl I'm interested in is a professional fighter, same as me. She's beautiful, fierce, and won't let me off the hook for anything."

"Sounds as if I'd like her," Dad says. "When are you bringing her to visit?"

I savor a mouthful of coffee before replying. "Once I win her over. At the moment, I haven't gotten there yet. She's a very cautious person and might have been burned before, so I need to let her know she can trust me."

"Don't rush her," Mom warns, raising a finger. "That's a surefire way to scare her off, and I want the chance to meet this girl."

"You'll get it," I promise, wishing I felt as sure as I sound. I dearly want to believe Harley will come around, but while I'm certain she's attracted to me, that doesn't always mean something in the grand scheme of things. Gabe and Sydney shared a mutual attraction for years before they acted on it. The thought of going for that long without touching Harley sets my teeth on edge. "Now, tell me what's going on with you."

# Chapter Six

*HARLEY*

Once I've showered and changed into a fresh set of clothes, I take an Uber to Jase's house. I pause outside for a few moments to take it in. The place is big, modern, and looks expensive. It's hard to picture Jase, with his tattoos and cocky smirk, being at home here. But maybe there's a side to him I haven't seen yet. I wander down the drive and knock on the door. A few seconds later, it swings inward, and I look into a pair of the brightest blue eyes I've ever seen.

"Uh, hi." I stick out a hand. "You must be Lena."

The woman, who has clear skin and red hair, breaks into a smile. "And you must be Harley. It's so nice to meet you." She takes my hand and gives it a shake, then holds onto it for a beat longer and squeezes. "I'm glad you came. Things can get a bit overwhelming with all the testosterone at the gym and we figured you could use a break from it by now. Come on in." She stands aside. I stop in the doorway to kick off my shoes. "Oh, don't worry about that."

"Thanks for inviting me," I say, lining my footwear

up against the wall regardless of her comment. I'm not traipsing dirt into this McMansion. "I'm used to the testosterone at this point in my life, but I don't really know anyone in Vegas so it can be a bit lonely." Especially when I'm used to being surrounded by people twenty-four-seven and suddenly the only person around me is Seth, who doesn't talk much. I hold up the container that was tucked under one of my arms. "I brought healthy snacks because I'm in fight camp. Is there somewhere I can put them?"

"Pop them in the fridge," Sydney says from a doorway that leads further into the house. She smiles warmly. "I made some healthy options too. Lena and I are used to catering for the boys, and we didn't want you to go hungry. Save yours for later."

"Oh." Well, now I feel awkward. Of course these women are used to fighters and their needs. They're *dating* them. "Thanks, that's really nice of you."

"No worries." Sydney's smile might be the loveliest one I've ever seen. I can tell why Gabe is with her. She's his perfect foil. Open and soft where he's quiet and broody. Not that I've met him in person, but we've talked a couple of times over the years. She tilts her head. "Come with me, and I'll show you where the kitchen is. Lena has already prepared a platter of finger foods in the living room."

I follow her into a mammoth kitchen with a long bench down the center and all the appliances a person could possibly desire. "Whoa."

"I know, right?" She takes my container and puts it in the refrigerator. "The boys are serious about eating well, and that means making sure they have the right equipment."

"I've gotta tell you, Seth's kitchen doesn't look anything like this. It's bare basics. Oven, refrigerator, freezer, microwave." But then, he's not the fancy type. Never has been, even at the height of his fame.

"What does his place look like?" Lena asks from behind us. I turn, and find her expression full of interest. "Neither of us have been. The guys might have, but they're not exactly into details."

I shrug. "It's your basic condo. Two bedrooms, bathroom, kitchen, and open concept living space. To be honest, I don't think he spends much time there."

"Hmm." Lena's eyes narrow and her lips purse in thought. "Is there a woman in his life?"

A hard lump of discomfort settles in my gut. "Other than me? Not that I know of."

I'm not sure how I'd handle it if there was. As far as I'm concerned, he belongs with Ashlin and always will. The thought of him with anyone else is just wrong.

"Okay, enough with the inquisition," Sydney says, giving me an apologetic look. "Seth is a bit enigmatic, so it's hard not to be curious."

Lena turns and heads away. Sydney follows, and I fall into step behind them.

"I don't think enigmatic is the right word," I reply. "He just doesn't have much going on outside the gym, so there's nothing to talk about."

"That's a bit sad." Lena sinks onto a sofa and Sydney takes an armchair. "He's a good-looking guy."

"Ugh." I pull a face, and sink onto the spot beside Lena. "Can we not go there please?"

She laughs. "Sorry. Like Syd said, he's intriguing. But then"—she grins—"so are you. It's not every day we meet a female fighter. What's it like?"

"Amazing," I answer truthfully. "I love it so much. I get to do my favorite thing all day every day."

Both women's brows shoot up.

"But doesn't it hurt?" Sydney asks. "Aren't you worried something will go wrong?"

Lena helps herself to a piece of cheese from the platter on the coffee table, and I reach for a carrot stick and dip it in hummus while I consider my answer.

"Yes, and no. The pain aspect isn't as bad as most people think. Your body gets used to the kind of impacts that happen during training. Shins toughen up and after a few months, you stop bruising so much. Sparring is usually gentle—at least, it was in Thailand, because people fight every few weeks and can't afford to be injured." I smile in memory. Some of my favorite moments have been spent sparring with friends. "It's almost playful, really. People over here tend to go a bit harder, but still not enough to do real damage, and during a fight, the adrenaline is so strong, you don't feel much of anything." Glancing up, I find that they're both watching me, enthralled. I laugh. "Sorry, I can ramble about muay thai for hours."

"Don't be sorry." Sydney rests her chin on her palm and leans forward. "We'd love to hear."

"What was it like living in Thailand?" Lena asks. "Was it different from here? Where were you based?"

I grab another carrot stick, warming to the topic. "I lived in a complex attached to a gym in Phuket, just outside of the more populated area. It was beautiful. Really hot, but the climate grows on you."

Lena whips out her phone and taps at the screen. A moment later, she brings up a picture and shows Sydney. They both sigh.

"It looks gorgeous," Sydney says.

"It is." A pang of homesickness shoots through me, tugging the corners of my mouth down. "And the life-style is so simple. At least, it was up until the end."

"If you don't mind us asking, why'd you leave?"

The question comes from Sydney, whose expression is cautious. "You don't have to explain if you'd prefer not to, but it sounds like you miss it."

Sighing, I tug a hand through the damp strands of my hair. I'm not going to tell these girls the whole story. I'm not sure if I can trust them to keep it to themselves, but I suppose an abbreviated version couldn't hurt.

"My coach asked me to throw a fight. I didn't, and he was furious and kicked me out. Not that I'd have wanted to stay anyway. I don't represent cheaters." Or sleep with them, either.

"Fuck him." Lena's eyes flash with icy fury. "What an asshole. You're better off without him."

"I know." But somehow that doesn't make it easier.

We sit in silence for a moment, and I continue to munch on carrot sticks, then Lena speaks. "Can you tell us more about what it's like to be a female fighter?"

"It's very satisfying." I wipe my hands on a napkin and sit back, drawing my knees up to my chest. "Don't get me wrong, there are challenges. I have to work twice as hard to get people to take me seriously, but once I punch them in the face a few times, they usually come around."

She laugh-snorts, and her hand flies to her mouth. "Maybe I need to try that."

"Make sure it's people you're allowed to punch," I warn. "You can't go doing that shit to just anybody."

Sydney snickers, and I can't help feeling pleased. For some reason, I want them to like me. I miss having women in my life.

Lena nods. "I'll keep that in mind."

"But yeah," I continue, "being a fighter is all I want. If I can make enough money to pay the bills and keep doing it indefinitely, then I'm happy. It's rewarding, and even though it's not always easy, there's nothing I'd rather do. Plus it's amazing for self-confidence. I wasn't what you'd call assertive when I started. I was used to Seth fighting my battles for me, but when he left, I didn't have much chance other than to start fighting them myself. In the end, it turns out that's how I prefer it."

"Wow." Sydney is shaking her head, although she doesn't seem to notice. "That's kind of inspirational."

A blossom of warmth unfurls within me, and I duck my head, embarrassed by the praise even while I revel in it. "Thanks."

Lena steeples her hands together. "Would you teach me some basics? I want to surprise Jase."

"Absolutely." I grin. I love teaching martial arts nearly as much as I love doing them. "Except for training, I'm free any time, so just say when."

"Seriously? You're the best." She turns to Sydney. "Can you believe it took us this long to meet a female version of Jase?"

I roll my eyes, used to comparisons like this.

"She's more of a Gabe," Sydney argues. "A strong, silent type."

"Actually," I interrupt, holding up a hand. "I'm a Harley, and that's all I need to be."

"Even better." Lena looks positively gleeful. "Devon is in over his head with you. I can't wait to see you put him in his place. He's way too sure of himself."

My brows pinch together. "What do you mean?"

"Uh, Lena." Sydney clears her throat. "Aren't you getting ahead of yourself?"

"Doubt it." She reaches for a glass of wine and sips. "You must know that Devon has a thing for you, right? He's not exactly subtle."

Squirming in the seat, I wonder if it's physically possible for my cheeks to be as red as they feel, because they're fucking scorching. I'm not used to this kind of girl talk, and I don't know what a normal response would be.

"You're making her uncomfortable." Sydney's smile is gentle. "Ignore her. We're just not used to seeing Devon twisted up like this over a girl. He's more the love 'em and leave 'em type."

"I know," I reply, grateful both for the explanation and the reprieve. "It's kind of obvious." Turning to Lena, I add, "You're right that he's made it clear what he wants, but I'm not looking to be the girl who ropes him. I'm nobody's exception to the rule, and if I went there, I'm sure he'd have moved on within a week. Besides"—I go for the knockout blow—"Seth is helping me restart my life, and his good opinion matters."

"So you're saying you'll keep your hands off Devon?" she clarifies, her lips pursed with disappointment. "And here I was hoping to see him fall hard and fast."

"Not for me." I examine my fingernails. They're short and neat. Unfeminine. Hardly worthy of a seductive vixen like Devon seems to think I am. If he ever got me where he wanted, he'd soon grow bored. "Trusting people isn't something I'm good at, and he has this wild energy that screams unreliable."

Lena sighs. "Oh, well. I suppose I can't argue with you there."

Sydney grabs a remote and flicks the TV on. "Shall we watch the fights? They should be starting soon."

*DEVON*

I stand on the edge of the crowd, just inside the arena, and watch the action going on in the cage. Jimmy has just finished his fight and I'm officially off-duty as one of his cornermen. Not that I had to do anything more than ice his legs and back. Seth does the hard yards, watching every move and offering advice—or really loud motivation—between rounds. He sees things I don't notice, no matter how hard I try, but I still attempt to guess what he's going to say because one day, I want to be the one coaching younger fighters. I'm not stupid. I can't be a professional athlete forever, but I can be a coach. There's no age limit on that. No physical limitations either, so it doesn't matter how banged up I get along the way.

My phone buzzes in my pocket. Beside me, Jase is flat-out messaging Lena, and Gabe left the moment Jimmy's fight ended to return to Sydney. Seth is probably still debriefing Jimmy somewhere in a back room. I grab my phone from my pocket and check the screen. It's an unknown number. I tap the message, opening it.

Unknown: *Hey. We saw you and Seth on TV. Having fun? - Harley*

Grinning, I rub the back of my neck with my free hand. She must have gotten my number from one of the girls, which means she put in the effort to find it. She wants to talk.

Yeah, sweetheart, I'm down to talk.

Devon: *Lots. What did you think of the fight?*

Jase pushes away from the wall and shoves his hands in his pockets. "I'm off, bro. Don't do anything crazy."

"When have I ever?"

He raises a brow at that. "Every damn day. See you."

"Catch you."

My phone pings again and I hurry to see what she sent.

Harley: *Good fitness but a bit too slow on the defense. His low kicks were destroying the other guy but he should try mixing it up with body and head kicks. From what I could tell, the ground work looked good.*

My grin broadens. Seriously, how freaking awesome is it to have this conversation with a hot girl? Especially when she's spot on. I noticed the same thing about his reaction times and preference for leg kicks.

Devon: *Needs to improve his flexibility. His body kicks are fine, but he has a hard time getting his leg high enough to go for head kicks.*

Not a problem Harley has, I've noticed. She can execute a flawless roundhouse kick to the face and land back in fight stance with perfect balance. It's sexy as fuck. Especially when her lips curl into that arrogant smirk that says she knows exactly what she's capable of. My dick twitches in my pants, but fortunately decides to chill out.

Harley: *I can work on that with him.*

My first thought is: I'd like to see that. My second is a flash of brilliance that I'm amazed I didn't think of earlier. She turned down a date with me, but what if it wasn't a date? What if it was a reconnaissance mission for her upcoming elimination tournament? We could watch the other girls fight and dissect them like we're doing now. Meanwhile, we'd be spending time together. Growing closer. And I could prove to her that I can be more than a good-time guy.

It's genius.

"What's that massive grin about?" Seth asks as he comes up beside me.

Crap. Immediately, I wipe it off my face. I hate

55

being sneaky around him, but I don't want to fess up until there's actually something to confess to—except for having a few fantasies, which is hardly anything he wants to know anyway.

"Just a girl I'm texting," I answer, which isn't technically a lie. Still, it isn't the way I like to operate. I'm an open book, and that's how I prefer it. There have been enough untruths in my life without me adding to them.

"Right." He's not interested in knowing more. If he had any idea what's going on in my mind, he wouldn't be so relaxed. "I'm gonna stay to watch the last couple, then head off. You?"

"Same here."

He cocks his head, giving me a hard stare. "You're not hanging around to pick up a woman?"

"Nope."

As if on cue, one of the ring girls—a petite brunette with disproportionately big tits—emerges from the door behind us and sidles over. I recognize her from the rotating collection of people to grace my bed, but I'm coming up blank on a name. Something a little wild-child, I think. Serenity, Breeze, Willow maybe.

"Hey, Dev." She slides a hand over my chest, and I step back so it falls away. Going up on tiptoes, she whispers in my ear, "I'm free all night, and I miss your cock."

Said cock is limp as a cooked noodle, despite her breathy offer. Apparently, it's only interested in feisty fighters these days.

"Thanks, but not tonight." I take another step toward Seth, and jerk my thumb at him. "Me and the big guy have work to do."

"Aw." She pouts. "Come find me if you change

your mind."

"Will do."

As soon as she goes, Seth snorts. "Not interested in round two?"

"Nah. Got other things to do."

He gives me a strange look, and I can't say I blame him. It's rare for me to prioritize anything over training or having a good time. Unfortunately, I can't explain that I don't want to touch any woman who isn't his sister. Jesus, imagine how that would go down.

We watch the last two fights in companionable silence and then part ways. I drive back to my apartment, eager to be alone so I can put my plan into action. I jog up the stairs, unlock my door, and head for the bedroom. Stripping off my shirt, I look in the mirror and evaluate what I see there. Short black hair. Dark skin. Awesome-as-hell abs. I give myself a thumbs up.

"You got this, man."

I flop back on the bed, select Harley's number, and hit the call button. It rings and rings and she doesn't pick up. For the first time, it occurs to me that she might not answer. And then what? I suppose there's a chance I'll see her at the gym tomorrow, but Sundays are a rest day for most people. Finally, just as I'm about to give up, the call connects.

"Hey." Her voice is husky, as if she's trying to whisper. "Had to get into my bedroom before I could answer, so Seth can't eavesdrop. What's up?"

"There's an event on next weekend. Steel Angels. Some of the girls competing in your tournament are fighting in it. Want to come along and watch?" I suck in a breath and cross my fingers.

She's quiet for a moment. "With you?"

"Yeah." I roll my eyes, inwardly berating myself for

not making it obvious. "I have some tickets and need company, so I thought of you." I don't have tickets. It's a total lie. But I forgive myself for it because I'll get my hands on some first thing tomorrow and she'll never know the difference.

She hums in thought. I can tell she's tempted, and I let the offer hang in the air. I'm not stupid enough to say something else and risk blowing it. I've put it out there, and it's up to her to take the next step.

"Okay," she says on a sigh. "That would actually be good preparation, but I have a condition."

"Anything."

Yep, that's me, playing it cool like a boss.

"It can't be just you and me. This is not a date."

"Done." I'll get enough tickets for Jase and Gabe, and they can be my wingmen. Assuming they don't rat me out to Seth first. But then, why would they? This isn't a date. I grin, practically gleeful. "Can't wait. I'll text you the details."

"Great." She hesitates for a moment, then adds, "Thanks. I'm not sure whether Seth would have mentioned it. He's got this thing about not worrying me ahead of time. He thinks I'll see what pros they are with the grappling and freak out, but honestly, that's not my style. I need to know what I'm dealing with so I can be prepared, and with seventy-six fights under my belt, it's not as if I don't have a fairly good idea of what's coming."

This may be the most words she's ever said to me in one go.

"You're welcome. And can I just say how fucking awesome it is that you've had seventy-six fights? I might not have that many in my entire career but you have before you're even thirty."

She makes a dismissive sound. "Seventy-six is

nothing compared to some of the fighters in Thailand. I trained with guys who had three or four hundred."

"Whoa." I whistle. "Okay, you're right. You've got nothing on them."

A laugh bursts from her, almost as though it's caught her by surprise, and my heart stutters in response. "I didn't expect you to agree with me!"

Grinning, I roll onto my side. "Shouldn't say things if you don't mean them."

Still chuckling, she replies, "Yeah, okay. I guess I thought you were a shameless flirt who'd say anything. No offense."

"Offense taken, Harls."

"No one calls me that." I can picture her shaking her head. "'Harley' is not the kind of name you shorten."

My lips twitch. Challenge accepted. "Just watch me."

She sighs. "I'd better go. Thanks for the invite. I'll see you Monday."

"Big plans for the weekend?" I ask, clutching the phone tight to my ear, not wanting her to end the call.

This time, her sigh is heavy. "Shopping for clothes. I don't really have much that's not activewear, seeing as I lived at a gym and all, so I've got a few essentials to pick up."

"That doesn't seem like your kind of thing."

"It's not, but you gotta do what you gotta do." She doesn't ask about my plans, and I find myself wanting to tell her. But then she speaks again. "Goodnight, Devon."

I hold all the words I want to say inside of me. They can wait for later. Baby steps.

"Night, Harls." I hang up, and pump my fist. I'm going to win my girl. It just might take a while.

## Chapter Seven

*Devon*

First thing on Monday morning, I get my hands on six tickets to the Steel Angels fight night, then message Gabe and Jase in our group chat.

Devon: *Got some tickets to Steel Angels. You and your girls want to come?*

The perfect idea struck me this morning. Triple date. Technically, it's just a group of friends going to an event together, but with everyone partnered off—and both Jase and Gabe unable to leave their better halves alone for more than a few minutes without wanting to bust the heads of any guys who look their way—Harley will be left with me. It's the perfect chance to get to know her better.

Jase: *We're in. Lena is really interested in female fighters after meeting Harley.*

Oh, yeah. It had slipped my mind that she spent Saturday night with Lena and Sydney. I wonder how that went. I hope they were nice to her. Knowing Sydney, I'm sure they were all that's sweetness and rainbows. Lena's a bit more fiery, but Sydney has a gift for making everyone feel welcome and like they belong. Gabe doesn't reply for another half hour, by which time I've run five miles and am about to head to the gym.

Gabe: *Random offer. Where'd you get them?*

Devon: *Jim Wiley. He's one of the sponsors.*

Gabe: *He just happened to give them to you?*

Devon: *I bought them.*

Ugh, why does he have to ask so many questions? He's a suspicious son of a bitch.

Jase chimes in as I head downstairs.

Jase: *Fuck, bro. Tell me this isn't about Harley.*

Devon: *Maybe it's a little bit about Harley. But come on, some of the girls in her tournament are taking part. In her shoes, any of us would want to go.*

Jase: *Yeah, okay. But don't make us regret it.*

Devon: *I won't. Gabe, you in, big guy?*

Gabe: *Someone needs to make sure you keep your hands to yourself.*

Devon: *Appreciate you looking out for me.*

Pocketing my phone, I spend the rest of the trip to the gym thinking about Harley and how her voice sounded in my ear late at night. Like she was on the bed with me. My heart swells. If I have my way, her voice will be the last thing I hear before I go to sleep every night. When I arrive, I head inside and take off my shoes. Jase is already here, and he's working with Harley, his head ducked close to hers. He's gesturing with his hands, and then he lays them on her and demonstrates a judo throw. She lands softly, rolls, and springs back to her feet. Her movements are graceful, and I could watch them forever.

"Dev." I flinch, and spin around to see Seth standing beside me. He holds up a padded hand. "You warmed up?"

"Did a run before I came. If you give me two minutes, I'll get everything loose again."

"Good." He nods firmly. "Need to work on your switch kicks."

"Great, be there in a mo." I wrap my hands quickly, skip for a few minutes, stretch, then make my way over to the octagon in the back, where Seth is shadow boxing while he waits. When he sees me coming, he slips the pads over his arms and paces to the middle of the ring. I hoist myself up to join him, and steady myself, then cross to where he's holding the pads and snap my left leg up in a powerful kick.

"Fake knee to switch," he barks. I comply.

For the next twenty minutes, he drills me until my leg is ready to collapse, then instructs me to punch a bag for a while so I don't burn my lower body out. While I do, I watch Harley. She's holding pads for Buster—a massive white guy with a crooked nose and no neck. She handles him like a goddamn pro, and based on how red his face is and the way his entire body heaves as he struggles to catch his breath, he's giving it his all in an attempt to impress her.

She does not look impressed.

On the contrary, she seems impatient with his posturing and any time he pauses, she indicates for him to throw a punch.

A smile curves my lips. She's not into beefy guys with no cardiovascular endurance. Given that I'm the complete opposite of Buster—leaner, darker, and quicker—I can't help but be heartened by that.

"Yo, Dev," Jase mutters as he passes by. "Eyes on the bag."

With difficulty, I tear my attention from Harley. Damn it, I can't be so obvious about my infatuation or Seth will notice. Settling into my groove, I throw straight punches, hooks, and uppercuts, working on technique rather than power. The round ends, and I can't resist another glance over. Harley has left Buster and is walking toward her water bottle.

I intercept her. "Hey, Harls."

She rolls her eyes. "I told you, no one shortens my name. It's weird."

"Well, now I do."

She continues toward her bottle, and I fall into step.

"Do you want your ticket, or should I hold onto it and pick you up on Saturday?"

"Now would be good." She grabs her drink and tosses her head back as she swallows. Sweat glistens on her throat and upper chest, and suddenly my mouth is dry. She puts the bottle down and wipes her face on a towel. "I'll just meet you at the venue. Save you having to go around and collect everyone."

"Okay." I'd much rather pick her up and have time alone with her, but I claimed this wasn't a date, so I can't exactly argue. I try to grin like I couldn't care less, but the look she gives me implies I'm not successful. "Wait right here and I'll get the ticket for you."

---

*Harley*

The week passes faster than I expect, and before I know it, Saturday has rolled around and I'm standing in my bedroom trying to figure out what to wear like it's a goddamn first date. Except I made it clear to Devon that it's not a date, so I don't know why I'm so wound up. It's ridiculous. And yet I can't help running my finger over the silky skirt of a dress I bought last weekend and wondering what he'd think of me in it.

The length makes it perfect to rest across the middle of my thighs. If I paired it with heels, my legs would look amazing. Is he a leg guy?

*Not. A. Date.*

But it's hard to remember that when the sparks have been flying between us all week. Every time we touch—which is often, since we're training buddies—I lose a few more of my brain cells and feel like a hormonal teenage girl. The other day, he cracked a joke, and I giggled. I fucking *giggled* in a gym full of muscle-bound men.

It's shocking that Seth hasn't noticed. My poker face might be decent, but Devon's is appalling. Several times a day, I catch him undressing me with his eyes, and perhaps I could ignore it if he was less charming and outrageously hot, but for some reason, he gets to me.

In a fit of defiance, I yank open a drawer, grab a pair of yoga pants and a Crown MMA zip-up hoodie, and change into them. There's no way he can possibly interpret it as a date now. Except, you know, I leave my belly bare, with only a sports bra beneath the hoodie because I'm still a woman and I'm allowed to be a little vain. I zip the hoodie, slip my purse and phone into my pocket, and stride through the apartment, hoping Seth will be in his bedroom. No such luck.

"Bye," I say, waving as I pass him on the sofa as I head for the door.

"Where are you going?" he asks, glancing over.

"Just out with some people from the gym."

"Oh, yeah?" He frowns, and it occurs to me that he might be disappointed he wasn't invited. "Who?"

"Just a couple of the guys. We're going to watch Steel Angels." I add that last part because I know it will distract him from exactly who I'm spending time with.

"You're scoping out the competition." He smiles wryly. "Guess it was too much to hope that you not look into them."

"Does it bother you that I'm going?" I'll do it whether he likes it or not, because I'm the sort of person who needs to know exactly what I'm facing, but I'd prefer not to have him unhappy with me.

He shrugs. "You're a good judge of your own process. I trust that you won't do anything to fuck things up for yourself."

A cold finger runs down my spine. I know he's talking about the fights and not my love life, but his words strike a little too close to home.

"I won't." I stride to his side and drop a kiss on his cheek, which is rough with reddish-blond stubble. His eyes—a shade of blue-green he must have inherited from his father—scan my face as though checking for some kind of tell. I squeeze his shoulder. "See you later."

"Debrief me," he says as I leave. "I want your take on the other girls."

I grin. "You got it."

Outside, I find an Uber waiting and take it to the venue—a club that's been transformed for the night. As I climb out, I fish my phone from my pocket and message Devon because I'm not sure who else he's invited to come with us.

Harley: *I'm here. Where are you?*

His response is quick.

Devon: *Wait at the entrance. I'll come find you.*

Doing as he says, I study the other people arriving. There are teenagers, men in ball caps, and women in cocktail dresses and stilettos. There are, however, very few dressed like me. I guess they're all out the back, waiting to step into the cage. The atmosphere buzzes with excitement. I love smaller venues like this because they're more intimate and the vibes are energizing. Everyone is pumped.

"Harley!"

I turn at the sound of my name. Devon is threading his way through the crowd toward me, and attraction punches me in the gut. I swipe my lip to make sure I'm not drooling. He looks *that good*. His dark jeans cling to his thighs like a second skin, showing off how muscular they are, and the royal blue shirt tucked into them sets off his lively eyes and perfect teeth even more than usual. The top two buttons are undone, and even though I've spent plenty of time staring at his chest, my eyes are drawn to the flash of dark skin behind the V of fabric.

"Hey," he says breathlessly, and wraps an arm around my back. "We're over here."

The seats he's claimed are in the second-to-front row. I spot four familiar people occupying them and grit my teeth. Jase and Lena. Gabe and Sydney. He's turned this into a triple date. Before we reach them, I come to a stop. He swings to face me and I narrow my eyes.

"This isn't a date," I tell him. "I don't care if you invite every guy at the gym and his plus-one. We are not on a date."

"I know." He shoots me his most wicked grin. "We're just a group of friends that happen to include three men and three women." He cocks his head. "You're not one of those people who thinks men and women can't be friends, are you?"

Damn him. He's putting words into my mouth, and I don't like it. But I also can't argue that he broke the terms of our agreement, because he didn't, and we both know it.

"Do you want to go home?" he asks, tugging at the collar of his shirt with one hand. "Have I upset you?"

"No," I sigh, because as much as I want to be annoyed, it's actually pretty sweet that he wants to spend time with me enough to orchestrate this whole thing. Maybe he does want more than sex. He's going to a lot of effort when he could easily pick up almost any other woman here. Instead of them, he's pursuing me, the queen of mixed messages.

"Sit with me." He offers a hand but I ignore it because holding his hand would definitely be date-like. I do take a moment to appreciate the strength of it though. The calluses and scarred knuckles show how hard he works. Heat shoots south. Dedication and a good work ethic are two traits I happen to find incredibly sexy.

We circle around the chairs and I smile at the others, then sink into a spot with Devon to my right and Lena to my left. Some guy on Devon's other side starts talking to him, and Lena ducks her head near mine.

"Did he set this up just to get close to you?" she asks.

I wince. "I'm starting to get that impression."

She shakes her head. "He's incorrigible. We don't mind shifting to put some distance between you, if you want."

"Thanks, but it's okay." She smells like berries, and suddenly I'm conscious of how I smell. Perfume isn't something I own, and the only fragrance I wear is in my deodorant.

"You want a drink?" Devon asks. "Beer? Water? Wine?"

"Water." I stand. "But I'll get it myself if you steer me in the right direction."

"I'll come," Sydney pipes up, and links her arm through mine before Devon has a chance to beat her to it. She winks at me. "Over here."

As we walk, she talks. "He means well. Honestly. He's a good guy, but he's totally full steam ahead when he wants something, and it's pretty clear he wants you."

"You think?" I'm not fishing for a compliment, I just don't get it. He's only known me for two weeks, and I've made it obvious that I won't be an easy catch. I don't understand why he's willing to go to so much trouble when he could easily have anyone else with nothing more than that panty-melting grin and a few words.

"Oh, yeah." We brush past people and force our way to the bar.

"What do you want?" I ask her as a bartender makes his way along the line of people to us.

"Anything white."

I raise a hand to catch the guy's attention. "A water and a white wine, please."

His gaze skims right over me and pauses on Sydney, lingering on her cleavage. I roll my eyes. See, this is the reaction I'm accustomed to from men. I might as well not exist.

"Water and white," I snap, waving my hand at him.

He shakes his head, looking dazed. "Yeah, whatever. Coming right up." He grabs two glasses and pours, then raises his head to check out Sydney again. "You here alone, sweetheart?"

"I'm here with my boyfriend, Gabe Mendoza," she replies, syrupy sweet.

He swallows, and his eyes flick away from her, as though he's expecting Gabe—in all his terrifying glory —to materialize behind her. "Oh, right. Well, here you go."

"Thanks."

As we return to our seats, I ask, "Does that happen often?"

"Only when I'm by myself. Apparently I look like easy pickings."

"Hmm." Other than Devon, I can't remember the last time a guy hit on me. Maybe what Thaklaew said has some merit and I'm just not what most guys want. I sigh. What do I care, anyway? I'm a fighter. A professional athlete. Not a girl out for a good time. But sometimes it's nice to feel wanted. And that's why, when I slip back into my seat, I don't shrug off Devon's arm or react when the tops of his fingers brush my shoulder. The scent of his skin is intoxicating, with a faint underlying hint of Deep Heat, and I can't resist breathing him in. He shifts closer.

"The girls in the first few fights are new to the scene," he murmurs.

"Figures." Generally event organizers like to save the best for last.

We watch the first two matches in silence, but when the third set of fighters are summoned to the cage, I recognize one of the women from the photographs Seth showed me. Shaved head, snake tattoos winding up her arms. She looks scary, but from years of fighting, I know not to judge an opponent by her appearance. Some of the toughest women I've faced have been petite.

"She's one of them," I murmur to Devon.

He nods. "That's Savage Rose. She's a pit bull."

The fight begins, and it doesn't take long for me to

realize he's right. Savage Rose moves relentlessly forward, and her strikes never let up. She doesn't give ground, and seems to have an endless supply of energy. The match doesn't even go two rounds because she lands a solid punch dead center of her opponent's face and the girl crumples.

"*Man.*" Devon whistles. "Took her down like a boss." He glances at me, one side of his mouth hitched up. "Nervous?"

"Fuck, no." I'm buzzing just from watching it. "I can't wait to get in the cage with her." She's my kind of fighter, and I can already see her weaknesses. "She's not used to being on the back foot. If I push forward, she won't know what to do with me. I might be reading too much into it, but I think she's used to people being intimidated by her."

He cocks his head, lips pursed thoughtfully. "You might be right. Hell, I'm a little scared of her. But," he adds, holding up a finger, "I'm more scared of you."

My laugh catches me by surprise and turns into a snort. My cheeks flame. Talk about embarrassing. "So you should be."

He meets my eyes, and my stomach somersaults. Unlike the bartender, I have his full and undivided attention, and the appreciation in his gaze makes me feel things I ought not to. Tingles. Stirrings. Stupid little flutters in my heart.

Except for the novelty of being a white female fighter in Thailand, I'm used to flying under the radar. I get the feeling Devon won't let me get away with that. He's trying to drag me, kicking and screaming, into the light, and I'm not sure what to do about it.

Squeezing my eyes shut, I angle my face away, only to feel the heat of his palm as it settles on my thigh. His touch is light and casual but my skin throbs beneath it and it occupies my mind so entirely that I couldn't even say whether the woman entering the ring is blonde or brunette, and I'm looking straight at her. All of my being concentrates down to his touch, and when his thumb rubs circles on my inner thigh, I twitch in surprise. At least, that's what I tell myself it is. Surely the racing of my heart and rush of arousal are simply side effects of shock. Thank God there's a layer of fabric between his thumb and my bare leg, or I'd be burning up. A sigh eases between my lips.

"Good?" he asks, voice low and wicked.

"No idea what you're talking about," I reply, determined to keep my focus on the next woman to enter the ring. She's another from my tournament, and looks like the girl next door with doe-like eyes, more curves than your average athlete, a smattering of freckles, and light brown hair that's braided to the nape of her neck and tied in a low ponytail. "What's her deal?"

I sense him turn toward the cage. "Enya Sears. Everyone's favorite girl fighter. Humble, tough, and cute."

"Huh." For some reason, hearing him call her cute bothers me. It shouldn't. He's a playboy, and he's done nothing to hide that, but perhaps I like to think I'm the only female fighter he finds attractive. "Cute isn't exactly a selling point for a pro athlete."

"Isn't it?" he asks, turning back to me. "Want to bet she rakes in the dough from sponsorship deals?"

His thumb has stopped drawing on my thigh, and I finally dare to look at him. "Ugh, I have such mixed feelings about those deals."

He raises a brow. "Why?"

"Because sponsors judge people based on the package they present to the world, not on how good they are or how much work they put in. It pisses me off."

"Why?" he repeats. "It's not as if they're all over-looking you. If you tried, you could probably bring in the big bucks, too. I mean, you don't have that sweet and wholesome thing going on, but you're hot as hell."

I don't dignify that with a response. I'm not sure whether he thinks false compliments will butter me up, but there's nothing I can say without looking ungrateful or vain, so I clamp my mouth shut.

The fight starts, and to my surprise, Enya Sears is more than just a doe-eyed cutie. She may not be tall or bulky, but she's technically proficient and moves with the grace of a ballet dancer and the speed of a gymnast. Despite myself, I'm impressed, and excited for the chance to face off against her.

*Game on, Sears.*

Once it wraps up, nature is calling so I let the others know where I'm going and head for the restroom.

# Chapter Eight

*Devon*

The moment Harley is out of earshot, Gabe and Jase shuffle along and trap me between them.

"What do you think you're doing?" Jase demands, eyes narrow.

I feign innocence. "What do you mean?"

Gabe scoffs. "He means that you're putting your hands all over Seth's baby sister, and it's not cool."

I do my best not to squirm. "'All over' seems like a stretch."

"But you would be if you thought you could get away with it," Jase says.

"I'm flirting," I allow. "But I flirt with everyone, so what's it matter?"

"I think it's the intention behind the flirting that they're concerned about," Lena says, joining the conversation.

Great, now it's three on one. I glance at Sydney. "Where do you sit in all of this, Syd?"

"Oh, no." She holds her hands up. "Don't bring me into it. I'm Switzerland."

"But aren't you on the side of love?" I ask. "Because that's what I want with her. This isn't about a body in my bed. I could get that anywhere. She's different."

Her eyes soften, as I knew they would because she's still hopped up on love juice from her new relationship. "Once you show that with your actions rather than your words, I'll support your crusade for love, but at the moment, you're still the same guy who, only a few weeks ago, said that a relationship wasn't in the cards for him yet."

"Because I hadn't met *her*," I huff, frustrated that none of them seem to see my point. "I get where you're coming from, and I'll prove my sincerity to you and Seth. He won't stand in the way of love if he knows our feelings are genuine."

Gabe gives me a weird look, and I reflect on my words and realize I just said more about my feelings than I have in a long time. Maybe ever.

"Bro, you're toast," Jase mutters, and for once, I have to agree with him. Especially when I glance in the direction of the bathrooms and spot Harley talking to Karson fucking Hayes, AKA Jase's nemesis, and Lena's ex, in addition to being the biggest asshole on the Vegas MMA scene.

He says something to her, and she shakes her head, but he lays a hand on her arm anyway. She snatches the limb from him and starts to sidestep, but he blocks her path. Dark fury consumes me as I zero in on her expression. She wants nothing to do with him, but he won't leave her be. In two seconds flat, I'm on my feet and striding across the room toward them, with Jase and Gabe at my back. However annoyed they may be at me, neither of them want Karson Hayes anywhere near a woman, kickass battle princess or not. In this, they've got my six.

Arriving at Harley's side, I slide an arm around her waist and settle my hand on her hip. Karson's cold blue stare flicks down to my hand, then returns to my face.

"Hi, asshole," I say.

He jerks his chin. "This your girl? You should keep a tighter leash on her. She's a flirt."

Taking a deep breath, I suppress the flames of anger burning in my gut. We all know he's lying. A flirt is the last thing Harley is, and arguing the point isn't going to get us anywhere. To my surprise, she hasn't shaken me off yet, although she's not exactly leaning into me either. She just stands there, shoulders tense, glare strong enough to vaporize any man with a conscience. Of course, a conscience is just one of many things Karson lacks.

"She's not my girl," I reply. "She's her own person. You might have a hard time understanding that seeing as your head is stuck so far up your ass, but if you pull it out for a bit, you'd find that she could pulverize you without any help from me."

Harley stiffens, and it occurs to me she might be mad I've intervened. Too late to take it back now though.

Karson snorts, and his gaze drifts sideways, as though he's just noticed that we outnumber him and he has no backup. "Yeah, right."

"You wanna try me and find out?" she asks, raising her fists.

His lip curls and he looks like he's about to say something derogatory. For the sake of not making a scene, I cut him off. "It'll be less embarrassing for all of us if you just leave her alone."

"If you think…" he begins, but trails off when a blonde appears behind him and grabs his arm. She has wide blue eyes, full pink lips, and the kind of thick curves a lot of guys find sexy. Not Karson though. Who is this girl?

"Let it go, K," she says, tugging at his arm, a hint of fear in her expression.

He gives Harley a nasty scowl, then follows the girl away.

"Is that his girlfriend?" Harley asks. "Because someone should tell her what a creep she's dating."

"That's Camile," Jase replies. "His twin sister."

Gabe and I both turn to stare at him.

"Twin?" I echo in disbelief. "Why is this the first I'm hearing of it?"

He shrugs. "She keeps out of the limelight. I think she's shy. I only know about her because of Lena. Karson isn't one to share attention."

"You got that right."

Gabe and Jase start back in the direction of their seats, but I pause. "You okay, Harls?"

"I'm fine."

"Good." I turn away, not wanting to crowd her, and follow my brothers, hoping she'll be close behind. But when I sink into my seat and finally look over my shoulder, she hasn't moved. My heart sinks. Did I just lose my chance with her?

---

*HARLEY*

"Excuse me?"

Glancing around, I spot one of the ring girls—a petite Hispanic woman in a belly-baring crop top, who must have approached from behind. "Yeah?"

The girl—who looks to be all of twenty—leans closer, her dark eyes sparking with interest. "Is he your boyfriend?" She nods toward Devon.

"Uh, no."

A furrow forms between her brows. "Fuck buddy?"

"Again, no." Where is she going with this?

My bewilderment must show on my face because she smiles and explains, "I don't want to step on any toes, but he's hot as hell and it was cool of him to stand up for you like that." She blinks, her false eyelashes making her eyes seem even bigger. "Does he have a girlfriend?"

I sigh. "As far as I know, he's a free agent."

"Perfect, thanks!" She wiggles her fingers in a little wave and sashays across the floor. I watch her go, frustration tearing me up inside. When she settles her dainty hand on Devon's arm and beams at him, I want to rip her off him and stuff her in a coat closet, however nice she might be. Why does it bother me so much when he returns her smile? And why didn't I lie and say he was taken?

Gah! Life is so damn complicated. All I want is to do the sport I love somewhere away from my ex. I don't want to be enchanted by a cheeky grin and killer body all wrapped up in a playful package. I didn't ask for this. But when the ring girl throws her head back, laughing, and I have the urge to pull her silky hair, there's no denying it either. I want Devon for myself.

"You did the right thing."

My gaze snaps to the woman who's approached while I was glaring across the bar.

She offers a hand. "Lynn Nicholson. Nice to meet you."

"Harley Isles," I reply. "You too."

"Related to Seth?" she asks.

"He's my brother. Or half-brother, technically."

She chuckles. "You were an oops baby, huh?"

The question puts me on the defensive. "What makes you say that?"

"You're much younger than him."

"I might be older than I look."

She raises a brow. "Twenty bucks says you're not a day past thirty."

"You'd be right," I concede. "What did you mean about me doing the right thing?"

Lynn runs a hand through short hair that's streaked with gray. Her fists are both wrapped, which means she's fighting tonight. "Letting that cutie go after your man. Men only complicate things. Trust me, you're better off avoiding them if you want a good career in the industry."

"He's not 'my man'." I roll my eyes at how old-fashioned and ridiculous those words sound coming out of my mouth. "He can be with whomever he wants."

"Uh-huh." Her tone is skeptical. "We both know he could be your man if that's what you wanted." She smirks. "He had that look about him, so don't even try to deny it, sweet-cheeks."

I grumble, but don't belabor the point. "You know all about men, do you?"

She holds three fingers up. "Three weddings, three divorces. I know more than you can possibly imagine." She rolls her eyes. "More than I ever wanted to."

Curiosity gets the better of me. She looks like she's been on the fight scene for years. She must be in her forties at least. How has she found time for three marriages?

"What did you learn?"

She holds up one finger. "Men cheat." She raises a

second finger. "They can't handle a woman who knows her own mind." A final finger. "At the end of the day, they'll let you down."

She drops her hands and presses her lips together. Another thought occurs to me. One that I definitely shouldn't share: apparently, bitterness causes wrinkles.

"Wow. You've given this some thought."

Is this what my future looks like? Still alone in another twenty years, cynical and blaming it on the men I've known? God, I hope not. I always pictured myself marrying eventually. Not right now, but I have no desire to spend my best years without someone to share them with.

"I have plenty of time to think," she replies. "It's just me, myself, and I these days. That's how I like it."

"You don't get lonely?" I ask.

She shrugs one shoulder. "Yeah, but everyone does. Lonely beats heartbroken any day of the fuckin' week."

Suddenly, I'm not so sure I agree. I can't help wondering how bleak her life is. Does she go home at the end of the day and find everything exactly as she left it? Does she sit on her couch with a chicken salad for dinner and mull over everything that's gone wrong? Does she have pets, or is she completely and utterly alone?

I don't want to be alone.

I won't always live with Seth. I'm already thinking about moving out, but I have no friends here besides Ashlin, and Seth would be gutted if I moved in with her. If I try to keep my heart to myself, am I going to end up like this thrice-divorced fighter, only without all the sex I'm sure she's had along the way?

"I'm sorry, I've got to go," I say distractedly, and beeline across the room to Devon, who has already

79

gotten rid of the ring girl. Grabbing him by the hand, I ignore the questioning looks from the others and drag him outside and around the corner of the building, into a more secluded area. Then, just as he opens his mouth—probably to ask what the hell I'm doing—I stretch onto my tiptoes and kiss him.

# Chapter Nine

*Devon*

Oh, my God.

She's kissing me.

Harley freaking Isles is kissing me. Her lips are petal-soft, in contrast to her firm, toned body. They part on a sigh, and although I have no idea why this is happening, I deepen the kiss, sweeping my tongue inside her mouth, getting my first taste of her. She has a faint peppermint flavor. She must have brushed her teeth before coming out tonight.

Her body presses closer, and she winds her arms around my neck. I shiver, loving the friction of her nails on my scalp. Of their own volition, my hands journey down her back and cup the perfect ass I've admired from afar more times than I can count. It feels just as good as it looks. I'm not surprised. I've seen her use the squat rack like a boss.

But why is she kissing me? Why now?

Surely the opportune time would have been right after our run-in with Karson, so what's happened since then to change her mind?

I pull back, shaking my befuddled head. "Why?"

She scrapes her teeth over her bottom lip, uncertainty flashing across her features. "Because I want you. Don't you want me too? Or was that just some forbidden taboo bullshit?"

"I want you," I assure her, caressing the side of her face. "This just seems to have come out of nowhere."

She shrugs. "I changed my mind."

Her gaze dips, and I catch a glimpse of vulnerability that makes my heart squeeze. She's afraid I'm going to reject her. *As if.*

"Look at me, Harley."

She raises her chin, hazel eyes glinting defiantly. Fuck, I love that expression. My heart bangs inside my ribcage like a jackhammer.

"Kissing you is a dream come true."

With that, I reclaim her mouth. To my surprise, she softens into me, going pliant in my arms. I pictured her more as the type to battle for control, but I like this. It's as if she's allowing me to see a side of her that no one else does. Her tits brush my chest. One of my hands settles on the skin of her lower back, which is exposed by the outfit she's wearing. She probably intended it to be unsexy but it's been driving me crazy all night. I love the feel of her. I've touched her before, but not like this. In training, there are other sets of eyes on us and I can't slip up, but in this moment I can explore her satiny skin the way I want to.

She shivers and stretches, reminding me of a cat— all litheness and repressed energy. When she rubs against my dick, which I've been doing my damnedest to ignore, a groan tears from my throat. I'm hard as hell, straining against my zipper, trying to get closer to her. She freezes, her eyes meeting mine. Have I freaked her out? But then, slowly, she undulates her hips.

Teasing me. She does it again, and again, I groan. I'm doing my best to behave, but if she keeps that up, I'm going to lose my shit. When her hand goes to my belt, I summon the most willpower I've ever displayed and stop her.

Her brows knit together, and her swollen lips pout. "Don't you want more?"

"Yeah," I admit. "But not here in some dark alley. You deserve better than that."

She cocks her head. "What if that's all I want?"

"Nuh-uh." I step away from her. "You and me aren't a one-and-done kind of deal, and I think you know that."

"So you don't want to have sex," she clarifies, and my cock twitches from hearing the word "sex" emerge from between her well-kissed lips.

"Hey, now, I didn't say that." I hold up my hands, grinning. "Don't get carried away. I was thinking we could head back to my place. Unless there are more fights you want to watch?"

She grimaces. "Two more. But maybe that's just as well." Her haze of lust seems to be wearing off. "If we left, the others would know what we've been doing."

"And?"

"While I want to be with you, and I know this is a crappy thing to ask, could we keep it quiet, at least for a little while?"

My heart sinks. She wants me to be her secret? Honestly, that hurts. I'd happily march back in there and announce to the entire bar that I just kissed her in the alley, and then I'd get on my phone and tell Seth I want to date his little sister. But the look she's giving me makes me think that would be a very bad idea.

"Are you ashamed of me?" I demand. My fingers

are growing cold and I curl them into my palms to warm them. "Is this because I'm black?"

"No!" She looks stricken, and places her hands on my chest, directly over my beating heart. "Not at all. I promise, that's not it, and I'm so sorry for even prompting you to question that. The color of your skin has zero impact on how I feel about you, just as I hope mine doesn't affect the way you feel about me."

"What is it then?" I implore, because I'm starting to get a prickle at the back of my neck that warns me bad things are coming.

"I just…" She sighs, then buries her face in her hands and growls. When she looks back up, that vulnerability has returned to her expression. "There are two reasons, but I need to explain something to you, so you'll understand. Something no one else knows."

"I won't tell anyone." My voice is soft. "I promise." Whatever she's about to say, it's serious enough to get in the way of our budding relationship, and I won't betray her trust by revealing it to another person.

"I've had a lot of upheaval lately." She steps back and visibly steels herself. "My last coach, Thaklaew, asked me to throw a fight. I didn't, and he kicked me out of his gym. That's why I came here."

My intake of breath seems to echo around the alley. I've heard of people fixing fights. It's something we all know goes on from time to time, but it's never happened to any of my friends and the idea of her being kicked out of a gym she'd lived at for years because she wouldn't go along with it is awful. Those places become your home. Your family. I can't even fathom the idea of being barred from Crown MMA Gym. My training buddies—and even grumpy Seth—

are my brothers. It's the first place I've ever truly fit in. The only place I belong.

"I'm so sorry." I wish I could take her in my arms to comfort her, but she doesn't look like she'd welcome it. "I'm not sure what that has to do with us, though."

I wait while emotions play across her face. I get the feeling she's struggling internally.

"The thing is," she says eventually, "Thaklaew wasn't only my coach."

"Oh?" My grip tightens on hers. I hadn't been expecting that.

"He and I were...together. Had been for a couple of years."

"Wait. Hold on. Let me get this straight. Your coach, who was also your boyfriend, asked you to throw a fight, and when you didn't, he kicked you out?"

"But wait," she says dryly. "There's more."

My stomach bottoms out. Whatever is coming, it can't be good.

"He was mad as hell when I refused to go along with his plan and admitted that he'd been cheating on me for most of our relationship."

Oh, fuck. Poor Harley. That guy is a monumental idiot. What kind of man wouldn't treasure a woman like her?

"With who?" I ask.

"Lots of different girls." She holds my gaze but it seems difficult for her. "Apparently, he liked the idea of spending his life with me because of our shared interests, but what we didn't share was his desire to get some action on the side. I had no clue. When he ended things, he made sure to tell me all of the reasons I hadn't been enough to keep him from sticking his dick in someone else."

My jaw tightens. "What an ass. Blaming you for his shitty behavior."

"Yeah. Gaslighting at its finest."

I can tell she doesn't completely believe it. I take her hand and squeeze it. "I'm sorry you went through that. It's a crappy thing to have happen. But trust me, his actions say more about him than they do about you."

She extricates her hand, exhales long and slow, then drags both palms down her face. "I know that," she says, her voice small. "Logically, I do, but try telling it to my subconscious. I mean, we'd never talked about marrying or anything because I tend not to look too far into the future, but he was a constant in my world for years and then all of a sudden he dropped me like a bad habit and told me everything I'd believed was a lie."

Her lips pinch together, then she forces them to relax before she continues. "So, I guess what I'm saying is that my heart is bruised, and I'm having a hard time trusting this attraction between us. Add that to the fact I've moved halfway across the world and started at a new gym… it just feels like everything is up in the air. Seth is my constant. My familiar person amid all the changes. The only thing he asked of me was not to hook up with anyone from the gym. He doesn't want drama. And I don't want to piss him off if nothing is going to come of this." She gestures between us. "I need a little time to trust in our connection before we tell everyone."

Seth isn't the only person she has. I'm here for her too, and I won't let her down. But I can see where she's coming from, and if a little time is all she needs to let the ground firm beneath her feet, I can give her that. Just not indefinitely.

"You wouldn't lose him, Harls. He loves you. But okay, we don't have to say anything—yet. But as soon as you feel comfortable with us, we come clean. No more secrets."

Her eyes shine with relief as she nods. "Thanks, Dev." She drops a single kiss on my lips. "I appreciate you being so understanding. I know I can be hard to deal with."

I smile. "You're worth it." And it's my job to show her that, so she'll be happy to open up and believe in what we have. I nod toward the bar. "Let's head back inside." I reach for her hand, then stop short, reminding myself it's not something I'm allowed to do. Gritting my teeth, I acknowledge that keeping my feelings on the down low is going to be a challenge. I'm not a secretive guy. I wear my emotions on my sleeve, and that's how I like it. But for the sake of her bruised heart, I can rein it in for a while.

The rest of the night is torture. I deserve a gold medal for not having my hands all over her. I even keep my distance as we say goodbye at the end of the night. Now that I know she wants me, I can be patient. I don't need to tempt her the way I did previously. If I were to travel that route, I might scare her off. Make her feel pressured. Instead, I just wish for her to change her mind, say 'to hell with it', and come home with me. But she doesn't. The others are still around when we part ways, so I don't say anything, just hold her gaze and will her to understand what I've already come to terms with.

We're meant for each other.

Touching her feels like coming home. And yeah, maybe relationships are a new concept for me, but my heart knows what it wants, and it hasn't steered me wrong yet.

In my apartment, I strip off my clothes, brush my teeth, and flop onto the bed. I close my eyes, but I'm too wired to sleep. I need to let off some steam. My hand trails over my abs and down to my dick. All it takes is the memory of Harley's skin, smooth and silky, and I'm hard. I stroke myself once, then twice, wondering if beating off is going to be a common occurrence with her in my life. If it is, I can live with that. Rubbing myself raw is better than rushing her into something she's not ready for. Closing my eyes, I picture her delicate pink lips.

*Oh, yeah. They'd feel really good around me.*

In my fantasy, she takes me into her mouth. I thrust into my hand, and my thoughts are so foggy, it's amazing I hear it.

Knock. Knock. Knock.

My heart leaps to my throat and I drop my cock like it's burned me. Someone is at my door.

# Chapter Ten

*HARLEY*

I'm not an impulsive person. Let's just put that out there. But when I'm finally alone, and I'm left facing a long night with no physical outlet, I can't handle it. I message Sydney to ask for an address—because I trust her to stay quiet—then I get an Uber to Devon's apartment. Now, standing outside, I hope I haven't made a mistake. But the way he responded to me earlier has turned everything on its head. He was so sweet. So real. Maybe Devon isn't the guy I thought he was, and maybe I'm not the woman I believed myself to be because I sure as fuck don't want to wake up in twenty years, bitter and alone. I'm not stupid; I know the attraction between us isn't likely to lead to anything permanent, but if I don't explore it, then that's a certainty. If I give it a chance... well, who knows where it might go?

The door swings open to reveal the most gorgeous half-naked male I've ever had the fortune to set eyes on. My gaze slides over his bulging upper arms and follows deep brown ripples of muscle from his ribs to the waistband of his gray sweatpants. I'm about to shift my attention to his face when it catches on the prominent tent being pitched in the front of his pants. Holy shit. Is that what I think it is?

I mean, duh. How could it possibly be anything else? But my brain is struggling to work, too distracted by his very sizable bulge.

*I bet he's going commando under there.*

The errant thought pops into my head and I try to dismiss it. A masculine chuckle breaks my appreciation of his barely concealed package.

"Much as I love the way you're looking at me, do you think you could make eye contact? Might make me feel less like a piece of meat."

"*Oh,*" I breathe, snapping my eyes to meet his, a guilty flush working its way down my neck. Unfortunately, with my coloring, I blush easily. "I'm so sorry."

"Uh-huh." He gives me a cocky smirk that I can't even feel annoyed about because I was checking him out, and he knows it. "I can put on a shirt if it helps."

"No!" A burst of panic jolts me into motion and I take a step forward. "Keep it off." He grins, and I bury my face in my hands. "Oh my God, this is not going the way I planned." I'd hoped to be smoother and more seductive, but instead my typical awkwardness in intimate situations is leaping to the fore. I'm great with guys, as long as I'm not interested in them or have no intention of acting on interest if it exists. As soon as I open myself to possibilities, *hello* foot in mouth. That's why I kissed him earlier with no prequel. Much easier than slowing down to talk.

"What I meant to say," I continue, desperate to save myself from ridicule, "is that I'd rather you take off more clothes than add them back on."

His lips twitch and his eyes sparkle. Did I make it better, or worse? I can't tell. Moving aside, he gestures me in. Out of habit, I remove my shoes before entering.

"Can I get you a drink?" he asks.

"Only if the drink is out of your navel." Dear God, I officially made it worse.

A full-blown laugh gusts from him and I could swear it echoes in the space around us. Despite my growing humiliation, I laugh too because the sound of his is infectious. He's one of those people who sets the vibe for the room, and with just the two of us here, it's easy to be carried away by the rich melody of his amusement.

"I get it, I get it," he says, backing away from me in the direction of his kitchen, which is open concept and attached to the living area. "You want to bone me." Going to the cupboard, he grabs a bottle of whiskey. "Want one?"

"No thanks," I say automatically, even though it would probably calm my nerves. "I don't drink during fight camp." Although I'm not surprised he does.

As if reading my mind, he tilts his head, his smile turning wry. "I can see the cogs turning in that brain of yours. You disapprove of alcohol."

"Only at certain times." I don't want him getting the impression I'm a judgmental stick in the mud. "It just seems unimportant compared to other things. Is it really worth the risk?"

He shrugs. "That's for each person to decide for themselves. If you're asking me, I think life is meant to be enjoyed, and I like a nightcap every now and then. Does that mean I'm out partying and getting wasted every night? Hell, no. Otherwise I wouldn't have gotten as far as I have."

Nodding, I concede the point. "I grew up in a town that wasn't always kind to my family. A single mom who had two kids more than a decade apart is like crack to the local gossips. I always knew that people would pay close attention if I ever took a step out of line, so I found it easier not to give them ammunition."

He retrieves a single shot glass from a drawer and pours a small portion of whiskey into it. "Surely, training in the martial arts added fuel to the fire."

Now it's my turn to shrug. "Yeah, but it was safer than the alternative."

"Which was?"

I watch as he sips the amber liquid, the cords of his throat moving. The edge of the glass rests gently on his plump lower lip and for a moment, I envy it. I remember how those lips felt and I want them on mine again.

"Harley?" he prompts.

"Oh, yeah." I swipe a strand of hair off my face with more vigor than necessary. "Getting beaten up. I was an easy target, but once I fought back a couple of times, the bullies left me alone." I can't believe we're standing in his kitchen having this conversation. "This isn't what I came here for."

"I know." He sets the whiskey down and approaches me. I stand my ground as he places his hands on the counter behind me and brackets me between his arms. His eyes search mine. "But I'm still not clear on exactly why you are here and what you want from me when you said you're having trouble trusting in our attraction. How about you break it down and make it really simple?"

Tipping my chin back, I refuse to be intimidated by his size and appeal. I take a breath and slowly release it. "I want you to fuck me."

"Okay." He nods, as though his lips aren't mere inches from mine, his body so close I can smell a hint of aftershave. "But would this be a one-off fucking or is it the start of a pattern of fucking?"

"Well, that really depends on how good it is, doesn't it?" I say tartly, and the cheeky grin vanishes from his face.

His eyes smolder like dark embers. "Trust me, you'll want more. The question is, are you going to let yourself have it?"

Groaning, I glance off to the side. Why is he forcing us to have this conversation? Aren't guys usually just eager to get whatever they can and figure it out later?

"Harley." His fingers land on my chin and he steers my face back to his. "I'm not doing this with you if I'm interchangeable with any other man out there. Either you want *me*, and you agree to give me a real chance, or you'll have to go scratch your itch elsewhere." His lips pinch together. "Although I must say, I don't love that option."

"Oh, my God. You're actually doing this." He's holding out for more. While it frustrates me because I'm afraid to open up to him more than I already have, I respect his position. Closing my eyes, because it's difficult to think with his gorgeous self all up in my grill, I think it over. I like Devon. He's fun to be around, but we're opposites in a lot of ways. I don't know him well enough to be willing to risk my relationship with Seth. That said, after tonight, I can't help thinking I've misjudged him, and not taking a chance feels just as risky as putting it all on the line. I don't want to live safely and end up sad and alone.

"Okay." It's hard to say the word around my clenched jaw, but even though my eyes are shut, I can sense the change in him. His body relaxes and sways closer to mine, brushing against me in a few key locations that send sparks crackling over my skin. Blinking, I refocus, and the joy that seems to radiate from his every pore attracts me to him like the opposing end of a magnet. "Let's give this a chance. But," I add as he starts to dip his head, "it's just between you and me for now."

"Until you feel secure in our relationship."

The air above my mouth stirs as his lips move. Heat rushes to my center. How is it so erotic when he hasn't even touched me yet? His lips brush mine. Once, twice. Soft as a butterfly's wing. Something flutters in the vicinity of my heart, and I ignore it. My heart shouldn't be involved. Not yet. No matter how sweet his kisses are.

He pulls back, and our gazes lock. "I'm not going to fuck you."

Disappointment sours my stomach. Why would he put me through everything he just did if he doesn't want me? I try to shove him away.

"Easy, sparky." He lowers his voice. "I'm going to make love to you. That's what it will be between us."

My insides tie themselves in knots. "You can't just say that."

He cocks a brow. "But I did, and if that's not okay with you, you're welcome to leave."

*Damn him.* I squeeze my fists at my sides. Damn. Him. Why does he have to play with my emotions like this? Why can't he just let sex be sex?

*Because he knows what you could have together.*

"Shut up," I mutter to the voice in my head.

His face falls and he lifts his hands off me and backs away.

"Not you," I add quickly.

*Be brave, Harley. You're willing to get in the ring with three women on one night. You can survive anything. Don't be such a wimp.*

Before my bravado can waver, I grip his shoulders and haul him back to me. His lips slant over mine, and I attack his mouth with none of the gentleness he showed, both angry and desperate at the same time. He meets my aggression with a tenderness that slows me down. His tongue strokes mine, stoking the fire within me hotter. His hands mold to my shape, melting me like butter. Then he pulls back and presses kisses to my temple, my cheeks, and my nose, before burying his face in the crook of my neck.

"So, that's a yes to the making love?"

"Yes."

"Thank fuck."

Impressively fast, he moves to toss me over his shoulder. Automatically, I evade and counter, stopping just short of sweeping his legs out from under him.

He shakes his head in wonder. "Fuck, that's hot." He offers me a hand, and I thread my fingers through it. "Come on, you sexy ninja. Let's go to bed."

I follow him across the living area and into a bedroom that's far from what I'm expecting. Cream-colored walls, drapes a masculine shade of green. A door to a bathroom that stands ajar and through which I can see a hot tub on the far wall. There are a couple of closets and some clothes strewn on the floor, but overall it's minimalist and tidy. Hardly the den of sin I imagined. There's not even a box of condoms on the nightstand, although I'm assuming he has them somewhere.

"Surprised?" he asks.

"A little." I'm not too rigid to admit it.

Pivoting to face me, he sinks onto the edge of the bed, his knees spread as though inviting me to step into the V of them. "Wanna know what I was doing before you knocked?"

My gaze darts to the pillows, which are rumpled, and back to him. I press my legs together to quell the need to squirm. My voice is husky when I ask, "What were you doing?"

"Jacking off." One of his hands slips inside his sweatpants and even though I can't see it, I can perfectly picture it fisting around his cock. "While I thought about you."

"Oh, God." My pussy throbs. It's wet, and he's only making things worse. "Can I see?"

His eyes widen and his abs flex as he puts one hand behind himself and leans back, supporting his weight on it. "Yeah."

With his other hand, he shoves his pants down, and his hard-as-granite erection slaps his lower belly. It's dark and smooth and looks like it would feel amazing inside me. He curls his palm around it and pumps slowly, watching my face as he pleasures himself. I squeeze my thighs tightly together, moisture seeping between them.

"You like that," he rumbles.

"Duh." I pop one of my fingers into my mouth, then part my legs and slip it into my panties, slicking through the center of my folds. "I bet you like to watch, too."

A groan tears from him. "No fair. You're covered up, I'm not."

Smirking, I slip one of the fingers inside me. "Who said I play fair?"

"God. *Fuck*." He releases his dick as precum beads on the head. "Show me. Now."

I tut. "Demanding."

But I want to. I want to see the look in his eyes when he realizes he's as helpless to the attraction blazing between us as I am, so I shimmy my panties down, and I'm about to pick up where I left off when I pause, suddenly self-conscious. I don't know what Devon is used to, but I don't wax. Frankly, I do enough to hurt myself and I've never seen the point. I trim, but maybe he's used to landscaped Las Vegas babes.

"Keep going," he urges, all lust and unfulfilled horniness. He doesn't care. I stroke through the slickness of my own desire, marveling at how strange it feels to do something so private in plain view of someone else. The thrill of it has my pulse pounding. It's naughty and freeing at the same time. "Come here." He pats the bed beside him. "I need to kiss you again."

I ditch my hoodie and yank my sports bra over my head, rendering myself completely naked, and his eyes damn near pop out of their sockets.

"Where were you hiding those?"

Grinning, I glance down. I'm not well-endowed, but for an athlete, I've got more going on than most. I've never been one of those girls who feels the need to show them off. In a training environment, it's better if the men think of me as one of their own, and having tits in their face tends to ruin that. But now, I'm grateful for them.

I perch on the edge of the bed, my gaze drawn once again to his dick. He's stopped touching it and it bobs against his stomach with a life of its own.

"Keep looking at it like that and I won't even last until I'm inside you," he says, sounding strained.

I trace a finger up his navel, following a sprinkling of dark hair, and work my way to his face, then lean over and kiss him. His hand goes to my jaw and he captures my mouth in a hot, wet exchange that's all tongues and panted breaths. My heart rate shoots up and my pussy throbs again, demanding attention. His hand settles over it and I whimper. He swallows the sound and torments me with his fingers.

"More," I gasp as we break apart.

He growls, and I love it. "You're so fucking hot. This little pussy is going to feel amazing wrapped around me."

He lifts his finger to his mouth and sucks it. I gulp. Then he threads his fingers between mine and shifts around, pressing me back into the bed, my hands pinned above my head. I simply relax and let him climb atop me. There are times to fight for dominance, and this isn't one of them. Not when his weight feels so delicious, and his erection grinds into me, setting off flashes of white behind my eyes as it rubs over my clit. I nip the skin on the side of his neck, then lick it to soothe the sting. His hips jerk, then he stills.

"Don't stop," I urge.

"Just. Need. A. Moment." He grits the words out, and I squirm against him, unable to help myself. "Oh, shit."

"You should get that condom."

"Good plan." He rolls off me, flops his feet onto the floor, and rustles around in the top draw of his nightstand, emerging victorious with a foil wrapper. He tears it open, and sits on the edge of the bed as he guides it over his length. I get onto my knees on the mattress, and his brows draw together. "What are you doing?"

"Like this." I straddle his thighs and watch realization dawn. He grips his cock and I sink onto it inch by inch, taking him so deep inside of me I could swear he touches my heart. His hands journey around to my ass and I bite my lower lip as I adjust to the size of him. He exhales and his fingers tremble as they dig into my flesh. His eyes are nearly black with desire and I keep mine locked on them while I start to move, lowering myself up and down. I cup my breasts and pinch the nipples lightly. He sits back and enjoys the show, his breath growing more ragged. After letting me be in control for a short while, he takes action, thrusting his hips and filling me so full of his cock that I see stars.

"Oh!"

He does it again, and my head flops onto his shoulder. His arms band around me and he supports me as he drills my pussy. Having him hold me like this is unexpectedly sweet, and emotion clogs my throat. I want to be able to see him, so I ease back and rest my forehead on his. We move in sync, riding higher, each caress of him inside me driving us to the brink of wildness. We exchange breath and kisses, not taking our eyes off each other as our pleasure crescendos.

It's intimate. So fucking intimate that I'm tempted to squeeze my eyes shut and deny him this moment of connection because it feels like he can see all the way to my soul. But for some crazy reason, I can't bring myself to do it. Instead, the intensity between us builds along with the pleasure so I see the exact moment his expression becomes raw with need. He hammers into me over and over and I sob as a shiver wracks my body. I come apart in his arms, shuddering and moaning, clinging desperately to the emotional thread that binds us together. My orgasm seems to trigger his. He stiffens and growls, low and dirty, his dick jerking inside of me. On and on it goes and I ride him all the way through it, until his muscles finally loosen and he hugs me tight to his chest.

A strange emotion boils up my throat. I can't put a name to it, but it seems intrinsically linked with Devon and makes me feel like someone has been digging around in my heart, unearthing everything I've ever tried to bury in there.

"That was incredible," he murmurs in my ear, and gently disengages.

I climb off him and watch as he removes the condom and takes it to the bathroom. A few seconds later, he's back, and he stretches out on the covers, his glorious body making me tingle all over again.

"Come join me," he says.

I hover, unsure whether I should dress and leave, but he smooths a hand along my hip and guides me into position beside him. When I lie down, he slings an arm over my waist and kisses the tip of my nose.

"That was so much better than what I had planned for the night."

"Me too." I wriggle closer and whisper, "I'm not sure what the protocol is now."

He rolls his eyes. "There is no protocol. But if you're saying you don't know whether to stay or go, then stay. I want you here."

*I want you here.*

How often have I heard those words? Not often enough, because they flay me. Although I lived around my fellow fighters and friends at the gym in Thailand, I've always been solitary. I keep my own confidence, and I'm usually a take-it-or-leave-it personality. Except for my family, it's rare for anyone to particularly care if I'm around.

That must be why I kiss his full lips and agree. "Okay, I'll stay."

He nuzzles me, and I like it a little too much. Something in the pit of my stomach tells me I'm in a lot of trouble. On top of that, I have to hope Seth won't notice I'm not home tomorrow morning. He's an early riser, so I cross my fingers that he'll assume I'm sleeping late and leave for the gym before he realizes I'm not there. Surely I'm owed that much good luck.

# Chapter Eleven

*Devon*

One eye cracks open and the glare of the morning light almost blinds me. The drapes have been opened. I feel around in the bed, but I'm alone. Bolting upright, I'm struck by a realization. I'm *alone*. Did I imagine last night? Did I only dream of falling asleep wrapped around Harley's lean, perfect body, inhaling the scent of her hair while her languid limbs were tangled in mine?

Surely not.

Studying the bed, I notice it's mussed. I'm usually a calm sleeper—that's how I manage to have so much energy the rest of the time. Harley was definitely here, but she's gone. A clink outside the bedroom draws my attention, and I pause to listen. Through the bedroom door, I can hear faint noises coming from the living area. Relief seeps into my pores. She didn't do an early morning walk of shame. She's still here. Before she can get it into her head to leave, I pull on a pair of boxers and follow the sounds to the kitchen, where I find her at the counter, pouring granola into a bowl. The sight punches me in the gut. She looks like she belongs barefoot in my kitchen.

"Morning, beautiful."

A flush stains her cheeks and she doesn't look at me until she's covered her breakfast with skim milk. "You're a heavy sleeper."

I shrug. "One of my best qualities."

When she gives me her attention, her eyes widen as they greedily look up and down my torso. I smirk, and tense my abs as her tongue flicks out to wet her lips. Yeah, she likes what she sees.

"You're not dressed." Her tone is accusatory, as if she actually expected me to take the time to put clothes on before making sure she hadn't disappeared. Unfortunately, she *is* dressed. She's wearing the crop top and yoga pants from yesterday, and I can't help but be disappointed. She looks good in them, but better naked.

"Nope." I pop the 'p' with relish. "I see you helped yourself to my cupboards."

"I did," she says agreeably. "Hope you don't mind. I'm pretty accustomed to eating other people's food."

"You can eat my food any day."

She rolls her eyes but smiles. Behind her, the kettle boils, and she turns and fills a mug. "You want tea or coffee?"

"I'll make a coffee. The good stuff." But for now, I'm enjoying the sight of her in my kitchen. It's so fucking domestic my heart almost can't take it. This is what I want with her for years into the future.

"When are you heading into the gym this morning?" she asks. "I want to make sure we don't turn up at the same time and make Seth suspicious."

*Damn.* Just when I'm riding an emotional high, she has to go and say that. I sneak a peek at her. She's sipping a green tea she must have found somewhere in the back of my pantry, and it's difficult to read her expression. I can't tell whether she regrets being with me, but surely the fact she's here bodes well.

"Actually…" I draw the word out. "I was thinking we could play hooky. It's a Sunday, after all. The gym is basically dead."

She raises her eyes to mine over the rim of her mug. "But you usually train on Sundays, and so do I, whether it's dead or not."

"Today isn't a typical Sunday. Spend the day with me." I waggle my eyebrows. "You know you want to."

She snorts, and it's adorable. "If we both don't turn up, Seth will know something is going on."

There it is again. The mention of Seth. A sliver of discomfort lodges in my spine. I really hate this whole being secretive thing. It's not in my nature. I'm an open person because I know how much untruths can hurt, and Seth is my friend. Keeping shit from him seems all kinds of wrong. But it won't be for long, right?

"How about the morning, then? You can go in later and I'll stay home so it doesn't look like we've been together." I round the counter and go to her, setting a hand on each of her hips, which are slim and golden from the sun. "Or are you planning to dine and dash?"

She sighs as if she's hard done by but her eyes glitter with amusement. "Okay, I'll stay. Just for the morning."

"Awesome!" Leaning over her mug carefully, so as not to knock it, I press a kiss to her forehead. "We could go for a walk. See some of the sights."

"Or we could stay here." She places her mug on the counter, comes to me and wraps her arms around my waist, resting her head on my shoulder. "Have some alone time together…"

---

*HARLEY*

Devon's uncertainty is written all over his face. He likes the idea of going back to bed, but hates the thought of hiding away, and that makes him so much sexier because it means he's unlikely to betray me like Thaklaew did. I can't imagine a guy like him sneaking around behind my back, and that's an incredible relief. I'm lucky he's willing to humor me. I know I'm asking a lot.

I tilt my chin up at the same time he dips his and our mouths meet in a gentle kiss that slowly builds. I nip his lower lip and he angles his hips, rubbing his hard dick into the V of my yoga pants. His boxers hardly conceal anything and it's a miracle I've been able to keep my hands off him for this long. His tongue meets mine and he groans.

"Maybe staying in is a good idea," he says.

Grinning, I back him into the counter and go onto my tiptoes, letting him take my weight. He brushes those delicious lips over my forehead, and I'll never admit how much I love his tender kisses. Then, faster than I can comprehend, he spins us around and lifts me up, depositing my butt on the counter. He steps into the space between my thighs and I laugh, delighted. It's not often someone catches me off guard.

"Are you laughing at my mad skills?" he demands, pretending to pout.

"Admiring them." I cup his face in my hands and show him how much I like his moves with my lips and tongue. His breath is warm and sweet because apparently he's a freak of nature who doesn't get morning breath. As for me, I popped a mint from the collection I found in his pantry before he got out of bed.

He pulls away and steps back. "Eat your breakfast, before I decide you're breakfast."

"I have no objection to that," I tell him, but he shakes his head.

"No, we're going to spend time together that doesn't involve being naked. Let's actually talk."

My hand goes to my chest. "Oh, the horror."

Surprisingly, I'm not feeling bad about it. He's fun to be around, and after the rigmarole he put me through last night, I'm prepared for anything. Hopping off the counter, I land lightly on my toes, then grab the cereal and take it to the two-person dining table on the other side of the room. He makes his coffee and grabs a mixing bowl, which he cracks several eggs into. Next he adds herbs, spices, and a few diced vegetables.

"Omelet?" I ask. I'd expected him simply to have cereal like me, but I can't blame him for wanting something more exciting; the smell coming from the bowl is enough to make my mouth water.

"Not just an omelet. The best damned omelet in the world."

I smirk. "You talk a big game."

He pours the mix into a pan and turns to face me, resting his forearms on the counter. "There are five things I cook well, and I'm awesome at them. Everything else is a total bust."

"Good to know." Helping myself to another spoonful of cereal, I can't help thinking how much worse it tastes now that I can smell the omelet cooking. I have regrets. I should have waited for him to get up before eating anything, but I thought he might be one of those people who sleep until mid-morning, and I'd have fainted from hunger by then. My body needs regular fuel.

"What else can you cook?" I ask.

"Hmm." He studies the countertop thoughtfully. "I make a mean stir fry. Fried rice. Thanks to Mom, I can do a Sunday roast. Oh, and my mashed potatoes are fucking delicious." He purses his lips and twists them to the side. "Yeah, that's about it. How about you? Do you like to cook?"

"Yeah," I admit, even though it's something I keep quiet because it doesn't exactly go with my tough reputation. "I learned how to make traditional Thai food from the locals in Phuket, and I make it a few times a week. It's one of the things I most miss about Thailand."

He nods. "They do have great food." While I finish my cereal, he flips his omelet and then plates it. "Would you like some?"

"Maybe a little." I hold my thumb and forefinger an inch apart.

"No problem." He portions off a second small serving and joins me. We sit together and talk. Not about anything in particular, but the kind of stuff that people in a relationship ought to know about each other. Like how his parents don't understand his love of MMA, which must be difficult for him. My mom has always been supportive, even when it scared her. In return, I tell him stories about growing up in small-town Oregon, and about the places I visited while I was living overseas. We've long since finished breakfast and are lounging on his sofa trading fight stories when my phone rings. I glance at the Caller ID. *Seth*.

"Hey," I answer.

"Where are you?" His tone is terse.

"Uh." I widen my eyes at Devon and show him who it is. "Out with a friend."

"Oh." He sounds subdued. Disappointed. "Are you coming in to train?"

"Yeah, I'll be there in an hour or two."

"Good. You still have a lot to learn before your fights."

My gut twists with shame and guilt. "I know. Don't worry, I'll be there."

"See you soon, Harley."

I don't miss the emphasis on 'soon'. "See you."

Hanging up, I meet Devon's eyes. "I'd better head off or he'll be pissed."

He nods. "I'm glad you stayed this morning."

Pleasure and wariness war inside me, but pleasure wins. "Me too."

Soon after, I shower and leave. Seth is withdrawn at training. Watchful. I hate it. And that's why, when Devon texts later to ask me to come over again, I know I should say no.

But I don't.

Because even though it may mean I have poor judgment, the thought of being with him makes me giddy. Indulging in whatever is going on between us must be one of the worst ideas I've had, but I want more of his jokes, his touches, and his attention.

Am I screwed?

I hope not.

# Chapter Twelve

*Devon*

Candles? Check.

Momma's Sunday roast? Check.

Suit and tie? Check.

Okay, so maybe it's a bit much, but convincing Harley to date me properly will be a challenge and I need to prove to her that I'm capable of more than she thinks. I can be the guy she needs. Strangely enough, I enjoy preparing for it. You'd think spending a couple of hours in the kitchen and stuffing myself into a suit would be hell, but I'm having fun. It feels right to do something special for her, and I can't wait to see how she reacts. She isn't like anyone I've ever known, and I have no idea how my dinner is going to go down with her.

Perhaps my excitement is for that very reason. I'm an adrenaline junkie. I'm not ashamed to admit it, and taking this chance has the familiar hot buzz of adrenaline shooting through my veins. It's been an hour since I invited her over, and she should be getting here any minute. I light the candles in the center of the dining table, which I've covered with a white cloth, and pour two glasses of sparkling water, which she can always swap for flat if she prefers.

A knock at the door grabs my attention and I set down the bottle and take my time walking over, not wanting to give away how eager I am. While I want to show her I'm serious, I don't want to come on too strong and scare her off.

"Hello." I pull the door open and greet her with a smile. "Come in, beautiful."

"Hi." Her eyes skate down my chest, all the way to my shoes, and back up. Her brow furrows. "What's the occasion?"

I answer a question with a question. "Who says there has to be one?"

She purses her lips and I can see her wondering what I'm up to, but then she squares her shoulders and enters. One hurdle down. She trusts me enough to come through the door.

She stops short when she sees the table. "What's going on?"

"Dinner," I reply, closing the door behind her. "I made roast. One of my specialties."

She hesitates, then glances down at herself. I do the same. She's wearing jeans and a tank top. Low key. Casual. But she blows my mind.

"Is this a date?" she asks. "Because I'm not dressed for it."

"It's just dinner. There's no one else here, so who cares how you're dressed? I wore a suit 'cause I thought you might like it on me." I shrug. "Some women dig suits, and I need whatever advantage I can get."

She cocks her head. "Why is that?"

"Because the power dynamic in our relationship is unbalanced and I'm trying to even it out."

"Wait." She blinks rapidly. "You think I have more power than you?"

"Uh, yeah." Seems obvious enough to me. I've fought for every inch of progress we've made. "I want to date you, but you're not sure what you want. That means the decision is in your hands, and you have the power."

"Huh." She tugs on a loose strand of hair, which is damp and curling against the side of her neck. Even from here, I can smell her shampoo, fresh and fruity. "I guess it all depends on your perspective."

I gesture at the table. "Why don't you sit and tell me yours."

She eases into the seat, watching me warily, then picks up her glass and sniffs.

"No alcohol, no sugar," I assure her.

She drinks, then pulls a face. "Ugh, what is this?"

Covering my mouth, I try not to laugh. Her expression is totally disgusted. She sticks her tongue out. My shoulders start to shake as I lose the battle.

"Seriously?" she demands, with a hint of a grin. "What did you do to that poor water?"

"Wasn't me." I plead innocent. "It came that way." I go to her and hold out a hand. "I'll refill it with tap water. How's that?"

"Perfect." Her grin widens until it's fully present. And holy hell, what a grin. If I could see it every day for the rest of my life, I'd be a happy man. Maybe it's special because of how rare it is, or perhaps because of the tiny flash of teeth between her slightly parted lips. Whatever it is, I'm addicted. "I'm not fancy, Devon. You don't have to pull out all the stops for me."

I bustle into the kitchen, tipping the offending

liquid down the drain, then rinse the glass, and refill it from the tap. "Maybe I want to."

She shakes her head. "I don't understand you."

I pass her the drink and sit opposite. "Because you're not trying."

Her nostrils flare. "What makes you think that?"

I shrug. "I'm not a difficult guy to understand. I say what I think and I don't have anything to hide."

I grab two plates and begin to serve our food.

She glances up. "Need a hand?"

"No, I got this."

She waits at the table while I dish up roast chicken, potatoes, carrots, and steamed broccoli. I bring it back and set a plate in front of her, taking the other for myself. The cutlery is already laid out; she picks hers up and scans the meal.

"This looks really good." She raises her eyes to mine. "What other surprises do you have up your sleeve?"

"Just wait and see."

"May I?" She gestures at the food with her cutlery, and I nod. At home we always said grace first—something a young me struggled with, having absolutely zero patience compared to my parents, and it isn't a tradition I've continued. She tastes a piece of potato and moans. "This is amazing. I totally underestimated you."

"Glad you like it."

She smiles shyly. "Next time, I'll have to make you a curry."

My heart stutters. "Next time?"

"Mm." She sips her water. "Assuming there's going to be a next time."

"I think that depends on you."

"Not really."

My brows knit together. What does she mean? Haven't I made it clear that I'll go on as many dates as she wants?

"Explain." Which jolts my memory. "And then explain what you meant by that comment before."

Focusing on her meal, she talks without meeting my eyes. "You don't know me well yet, and I'm afraid you might not like what you find when you do." She brushes a hand through her hair and I want to argue that my soul knew hers the moment we met, but she's actually right. I don't know all of her secrets and troubles. But I want to. "I'm not always a fun person to be around. I'm an athlete. My life is training."

"I think you're fun," I argue. "And your lifestyle is part of what draws me to you. I never thought I'd end up with anyone until after I retire because how would I fit them into my life? But you and I fit perfectly. We're both obsessed with our careers."

She nods, acknowledging this. "So is it just that I'm convenient?"

"No!" I shoot to my feet, knowing instantly that she's thinking about her asshole ex, then I take a deep breath and park my ass back down. "Of course not. I…" I trail off, figuring out how to phrase this without sounding nuts. "When I first walked into that gym and saw you, it was like I caught a glimpse of your soul, and it called out to mine. We might not know each other well yet, but I think that inside, where it counts, we're the same. That's not all, either. You make my heart beat like crazy every time you're near, and you're so fucking beautiful I can't take my eyes off you. There's nothing convenient about that."

She blinks, apparently stunned. "Thank you. That's one of the loveliest things anyone has ever said to me."

"I mean it." I cross my finger over my heart. "Your past sucks. I think we can both agree on that. But perhaps it was the universe's way of bringing you to me."

She gives me a searching look. "Do you believe in fate?"

"Yeah, I always have. As best I can figure, that's why I've survived when I'm kind of accident prone. It wasn't my time to go. Do you?"

She blows out a puff of air, considering the question. "I never have before. I'm pretty much a cynic when it comes to most things."

Raising my glass, I tip it toward her. "I'll win over your cynical heart yet."

"You can try, Green." She nods, and it's the closest thing to approval I've had from her all night. "You can try."

# Chapter Thirteen

*HARLEY*

Against my better judgment, I'm beginning to *like* Devon Green. He's a far better listener than I would have given him credit for, and he went to the effort of preparing a delicious dinner that's going cold on my plate. I shove my fork into the potato and take a mouthful.

"I'm sorry I distracted us," I say after I've swallowed. "It's really good. Is this the roast your mom taught you to make?"

He nods, and follows my cue, digging into his own meal. "Yeah. She firmly believes that men need to be able to make a decent roast. If not, we might stay single for our whole miserable lives." He pauses, humor quirking his mouth, and adds, "She thinks you're a miracle because I've been single for so long."

My heart pitter-patters. "You told her about me?"

"Of course." Lifting his God-awful sparkling water to his mouth, he drinks before continuing. "My career choice is a constant disappointment and she's always complained that I never bring girls home and don't seem serious about settling down, so I mentioned that I'd met a woman who'd changed my perspective."

"No way." Searching for signs of duplicity in his expression, I find none. "I can't believe you did that!"

He pauses. "Does it bother you?"

*Does it?*

To be honest, knowing that I'm out of the ordinary for him makes me feel special. I shouldn't like it, but I do. A week ago, I probably wouldn't even have believed him.

"No," I admit, opting to carry on my streak of honesty. I'm not good at being vulnerable, but he's putting himself out there for me and I want to do the same in return. "I like knowing what's going on in your head. I didn't have that with Thaklaew, and I know it's hypocritical of me considering we're keeping whatever this is"—I gesture between us—"a secret for now, but your openness is really attractive."

He grins, pleasure dancing in his dark eyes. "Did you just call me sexy?"

"Your attitude is sexy," I correct. "But yeah, the rest of you is all right, too."

"Damn straight."

He looks so smug I'm tempted to take it back, but it's the truth. He's allowed to be a little self-satisfied. I eat the last of my vegetables and set my cutlery down.

"What do you want out of life?" I ask. "More than anything."

He cocks his head, appearing surprised by the question. "I want to enjoy myself. To really *live*."

"That's it?" I ask. "No grand plans or ambition for world domination?"

"No." His answer is simple and sure. He's given this some thought. "If, in living my fullest life, I happen to achieve greatness, that's a bonus, but it isn't the aim.

What's the point of life if not to do what we love and follow our hearts?" His smile becomes softer. "That's why I went after you even though I never thought I'd find love at this stage in my life. When the right thing comes along, we instinctively recognize it, and I happen to believe my heart is a lot smarter than my brain. That's also why I do MMA, even though it's not the cookie cutter career my parents would like me to have. My heart steered me down the right path. I belong in the cage."

"Wow," I breathe, impressed. What would it be like to have that level of confidence in yourself?

"What about you, Harls? What do you want more than anything?"

My first instinct is to shrug, but I manage not to. I don't want to be glib when he gave me a genuine answer. "Honestly, I'm still figuring that out. I want to be involved in muay thai in some shape or form, but except for that, I don't know where I'm going. I'm taking every day as it comes and hoping things work out in the long run. But I do know," I add, psyching myself up for a confession, "that I don't want to be alone. I'm not sure who I want to be with, or in what sort of capacity, but I don't want a lonely life."

He scoots around the table and takes my chin between two of his fingers. "You won't be alone. Whether you find what you're looking for with me or someone else, or even if you grow old with Seth, you'll have someone."

Scoffing, I avert my eyes. It's difficult to be vulnerable with him when this discovery is new even to myself. "Nobody can know that for sure."

"I do," he says, tapping his chest. "I feel it in here."

I laugh, but his face is serious. I wriggle in my chair, growing restless. The intensity of the conversation has been too high for too long and we need to take it down a notch. There's only so much openness I can handle while my emotional wounds are still in the process of healing.

"I should go."

"Don't." He captures my hand. "We can stop talking for a while. Stay with me."

I do. And when he leads me to the sofa, I plant my palms on his chest, push him down onto the cushion, and straddle his hips.

"Are you sure?" he asks. "We can just—"

"I'm sure." I shimmy closer. Our talk has wound me tight, and I'm desperate to release my pent-up agitation and regain control of the situation. Arching back, I rock on his lap, riding the dick I can feel hardening beneath me. His hands land on my hips and he groans.

"Oh, God. Harley." He lets go of my hips and buries his hands in my hair, lifting his face toward mine, angling for a kiss. I grant him one, swearing to retain the upper hand even as he kisses me more sweetly than anyone ever has, threatening to crack me open and expose the sensitive, tender thing inside me to the world. I'm holding tightly to the pieces of myself, panic growing deep within that I can't control anything to do with Devon. I'm in danger of losing myself to him, and once that happens, everything will crumble. I'll have no defenses left. How will I keep myself safe then?

Our kiss is all-encompassing. His scent—masculine with a hint of menthol—engulfs me, and the only sensations I'm aware of are his lips on mine, his fingers raking over my scalp, and the iron rod in his pants. He grabs the hem of my tank top and yanks it over my head. I unbutton his shirt and do the same to him, baring his flawless abs and broad chest. His arms band around me, supporting me as I grind on him, then they journey up my back to the latch of my bra and flick it open with one deft movement. I hate to think of how many women he's practiced on.

"Get out of your head," he murmurs, as though he can read my thoughts. "All that matters right now is you and me."

Gently, he takes one of my nipples between his teeth and flicks the tip of his tongue over it. I shiver. Why do I feel out of control when I'm on top and taking the lead? Is that just his effect on me?

"More," I demand, and even though he does what I say, the added sensation only makes me feel brittle. Even when he's giving me what I want, he's still somehow calling the shots. Or is that just in my mind? Am I seeing it that way because of how vulnerable he makes me feel?

There's one surefire way to fix that.

Sliding down his torso, I undo his fly, and when he raises his hips, I pull his pants down, leaving him in silk boxers. I close my mouth over the ridge of his dick and run my tongue along the fabric over it. He growls and shudders like a barely leashed beast. A sense of calm washes over me. I've got this. I'm not the only one falling victim to the chemistry between us. I'm not weak. We're both in this together.

Slowly, I drag down the waistband of his boxers, licking along the groove that runs from his hips to his pelvis, following it all the way to the neatly trimmed hair above his erection.

"You feel that, don't you?" I murmur into the skin at the base of his abs.

"You tease."

"Don't you?" I repeat, my mouth hovering above his cock.

His voice is ragged when he says, "I feel *everything*."

Thank God.

I take him in my mouth, tasting his salty head, his thickness between my lips. He flops against the cushion when I suck, his body somehow taut and limp at the same time. I swirl my tongue around him, and he squirms. Then I settle in. Kissing, licking, sucking. He makes carnal sounds and his hips jerk wildly. I never knew giving a blow job could be so empowering. So fun. I love the way he's losing his shit because of something I'm doing.

He stiffens beneath me. "Better stop now, Harls."

I rear back, confused. His mouth is hanging open, his chest rising and falling rapidly, his eyes almost black. My gaze journeys down the length of his body, all of which gives the impression of being on the brink of something, and when I reach his cock, I notice it's leaking precum.

He sees me looking and closes his eyes. "Gotta get myself together. Give me a moment."

*Oh.*

My tongue darts out and laps the precum up.

He shudders again. "Fuck."

Deciding I've got a good enough grasp of myself to ease up on him, I back off and strip off my jeans. I'm not wearing anything beneath. While I didn't intend to have a date when I came over, I definitely had plans of revisiting naked-town with him. His eyes are still shut and my hand dips between my thighs. I'm soaking. Apparently I have a weird power fetish.

Devon's eyelids lift, and his eyes boggle when they focus on me. He wraps his thumb and forefinger around his dick and squeezes.

"Get on it," he growls. "There's a condom in my pocket."

I go to his pants and find it, then I rip the packet open and roll the condom on. "How do you want to do this?"

His jaw tenses, and he keeps hold of himself with one hand while guiding me with the other, until I'm seated on him, experiencing sweet fullness. The exquisite sensation of him inside me. And then, in an unexpected display of strength, he stands—his hands spread across my bottom, holding me up—and walks over to a wall. He presses me against it and keeps one hand on my ass while the other interlaces with my fingers and pins them above my head. Slowly, he thrusts into me, and in this new position, he hits spots that no one has ever touched.

My vision swims. I bite my lip.

He moves again, withdrawing almost all the way before sliding back in. This isn't the wild and dirty fucking I expected when he positioned me against the wall. His forehead touches mine as he fills me and retreats over and over again with a maddening deliberateness. My first urge is to speed him up, but then I notice the determination in his eyes and decide to let go and enjoy the ride. He wants to make this good, and it is. So damned good.

It's then, while he's methodically driving me to the edge of insanity, that lightning strikes. I see the truth: I'm afraid of him. Of what he makes me feel. By keeping him at a distance, I've been protecting myself.

But I'm not a woman driven by fear, so I choose to be fearless.

I open myself to him.

Lowering my walls, I let him see all of me, and I

look at him. Really look. Not being afraid of what I might find staring back at me.

He hits that perfect spot inside me again and it's more than I can take. I come apart, eyelids slamming down, every part of my body squeezing and writhing as a pleasure more intense than any I've ever known claims me.

"Oh, hell." Devon gasps. "I can feel you coming. It's… it's…" He trails off, a groan ripping from his chest as he joins me. Somehow, he manages to stagger to the bedroom, supporting my weight without collapsing, and then he sets me down carefully on the bed, as though worried he'll break me. It's ridiculous considering how competitive we get on the mats while I practice my jiu-jitsu, but sweet, nonetheless.

He flops beside me, grinning like crazy, and raises himself up for long enough to smooth the hair from my face and drop a kiss on my temple.

"That was magic," he says. "We're magic together. You're really something, Harley."

"So are you." In fact, I'm beginning to think he might be the piece I've been missing. Is that crazy?

I won't tell him. It's too soon for that. But maybe one day, I will.

# Chapter Fourteen

*Devon*

This time, when I wake, Harley is still in bed. Her lips curve, and her eyes appear green. They're clear. Guileless. The same way they were last night when we whispered confidences to each other in the near-dark, admitting all but the most important secret: how we really feel about each other. I could sense her holding back on that front, so I did too, not wanting to overwhelm her.

I'm falling, though. Falling fast.

I could stare into her eyes forever.

"Good morning, beautiful."

"Morning," she murmurs.

"This is how all days should begin," I say, and brush a kiss over the end of her nose. "You and me. In bed. Morning kisses. Always."

At first, she smiles softly, but then her expression begins to shutter. A crinkle forms between her brows and even though she doesn't say another word, she's emotionally withdrawing. The flow of energy between us has been halted. Did I say too much? Get ahead of myself?

"I'd better get going before Seth wakes up and wonders where I am," she says. "I can't be MIA for two nights in a row."

"Can't you say you were at a friend's place?"

She sighs. "What friend? Other than the people I've met at the gym and Seth's ex, I know no one here and I haven't had the chance to change that. He won't buy it. I need to go."

"Okay, then." I sit up and rub the sleep from my eyes. "But can I at least get you a coffee?"

"No time." She throws the blankets off and dresses in the clothes she wore over yesterday. By the time I pull myself together, she's almost at the door. I have to say, I'm not enjoying the love-him-and-leave-him vibe I'm getting from her right now.

"Whoa," I say before she bolts. "Hang on two seconds. Are we okay?"

"Yeah." She flashes me a smile, then drops a kiss on my cheek. "We're fine, Dev. I just have to go." A moment later, her blonde hair whips through the exit and she vanishes. I flop on the couch, feeling hollow. Damn. I need to be more careful. But most importantly, I want to know exactly what it was that scared her off so we can tackle it together.

A couple of hours later, at the gym, I ask her that exact thing. Her eyes narrow, her nostrils flare, and she gives me a look that would make a schoolmarm proud.

"Quiet," she hisses.

"I know," I reply. "But if you won't talk to me at home, then what else am I supposed to do?"

She glances over at Seth, who's rolling on the floor with Jase. "We don't need to talk. Everything is all right. I just needed to get back before Seth realized I hadn't come home last night."

None of this would be a problem if we came clean, but I keep that thought to myself because if I voice it, she'll probably push me away. The thing is, I don't think her brother would take it as badly as she believes, and I'm starting to wonder if maybe he's an excuse for her to keep me at a safe distance. She has every right to be hurting after what happened with her ex, but it's hard for me to reassure her if she won't admit it.

I sigh. "I'll leave you to it, then."

I steer clear of her for the rest of training, instead working through counter drills with one of the younger fighters and then sparring with Jase while Seth coaches us from the sidelines. Once or twice I notice her whaling on a bag like it personally offended her. Hopefully she can work all of the doubt out of her system by beating up invisible opponents.

I try not to watch her as she moves to the corner for a strength and resistance session, but there's only so long a man can ignore a beautiful woman if he knows what she looks like naked. When Jase clips me on the jaw during sparring, I totally deserve it for being distracted by her ass as she swings a kettle bell. He gives me a look, and I shrug one shoulder, acknowledging that I need to keep my focus on him instead of allowing it to waver.

Opting to shower at home, I head off without talking to Harley again, sparing us both the frustration, although I smile and wave on my way out the door so she knows I'm not angry. I figure she'll message me at some point. Four hours later, with no contact, I decide to take things into my own hands. Literally. If there's one thing I'm sure of, it's our sexual connection. We're dynamite together. It's only when things become deeper that she fortifies her walls.

Does that bother me? Yeah, actually. I want to be more to her than a body in bed. But that doesn't mean I won't take advantage of her attraction to me. That's why, after clearing the dinner dishes, I sprawl on my bed, naked from the waist down, close my eyes and picture her. I know, I know, it sounds bad, but I figure the way to tempt her back is by offering something I know she wants. So I imagine it's her slim hands instead of my own taking hold of my cock, and stroke. It thickens and stiffens, and in my mind's eye, I can see the way her eyes would darken, flecks of green glowing amongst the brown, as she plumps her lips and lowers them toward the head.

"Damn," I grit out, the image turning me on more than expected.

My eyelids flutter open and I grab my phone and flick her a text.

Devon: *My dick is hard and aching for you.*

In fact, I have to let it go and watch it throb against the planes of my stomach so it doesn't get too excited. For a while, I'm not sure whether she'll respond—was this a terrible idea?—but then I receive a message.

Harley: *My pussy is wet and wants you inside it.*

Devon: *Guess you'd better get over here before I finish the party without you.*

Nothing, for a long while, and I hold my breath. Then, finally, a response.

Harley: *Be there in ten.*

---

*HARLEY*

Why is he making this harder than it needs to be?

126

Why is he pushing when I'm not ready?

I need time to process what happened last night. I let my guard down, and it felt right in the moment, but this morning it struck me how vulnerable I'd allowed myself to be, and how much could go wrong. We're not guaranteed a happily ever after. It's not that I don't trust Devon's intentions—I do, mostly—but you know what they say about good intentions.

Unfortunately, it seems I'm helpless to resist him, so here I am, catching an Uber across town. I really need to fix my personal transport situation. Buy a car perhaps. Or an electric scooter.

I don't know exactly what's going to happen when I arrive, but if I've learned one thing with Devon, it's not to expect anything. On the face of it, this looks like a booty call, but for all I know I'll open his door and find a string quartet. A nice thought, actually, not that I particularly enjoy classical music. The point is, I wouldn't know what to do about it. He's challenging all of my preconceptions and keeping me on my toes.

I want to hate it, but the fact I keep coming back for more makes me think that's not how I truly feel. We stop outside his building, and I hop out and take my time walking through the halls to his door, afraid to seem too eager and tip the balance of power in his favor. I knock once sharply and wait for him to answer. When he does, he isn't wearing a suit. There are no violins. In fact, he looks exactly as I imagined he might when he texted. Clad in boxers but nothing else, the bulge behind the silk indicating that he's wound up more than his placid expression suggests.

"You're here," he says, and I can't figure out whether it's just an observation or if he's surprised.

"I am," I agree. "I hope you're prepared to follow through on those texts."

"Err." He rubs his chin as he gets out of the way so I can come in. "About that."

"What?" I'm suddenly suspicious. Are the violins about to come out?

"Here's the thing." He closes the door behind me and leans on it, his arms folded across his muscled chest. I'm about to make a comment about getting me here under false pretenses but then I notice the strain around his mouth and the hesitation in his eyes, so I let him go on. "I want to fuck you until you never think of another man again, but I'm not touching you unless you promise not to freak out when we're done."

*Freak out?*

"Excuse me?" I demand with more indignation than strictly required considering I know exactly what he means.

His lips press together, and he doesn't budge from his position on the door. "You're blowing hot and cold, Harls, and I think I know why. You're afraid I'll burn you. But I won't, swear to God. You're not the only one here with feelings, and I'm not sure I can handle being frozen out again when you get cold feet." His chest rises and falls. "It kinda sucks."

It does—I can see that—and I don't want to hurt him. That isn't part of my plan, but it seems to be a side effect of my self-preservation instincts.

"I'm sorry."

He nods. "Thank you. I didn't say any of that to guilt you, I just want you to understand where I'm coming from." He shifts from one foot to the other and drops his hands to his sides. "I don't only want sex from you, and if that's all you can give then it might be best if we slow down."

My internal reaction is an immediate and vehement refusal. Ending whatever is happening between us feels wrong. Strange, when I should be thanking him for the easy out and backing away before my heart gets more involved.

"No." My heart thump-thumps in an unfamiliar way, and I take a step toward him. "I don't want that."

He wets his lips. "Well, then, what do you want?"

"To believe you." The statement gusts from me on a breath. "So badly."

He glances up at the ceiling, and a muscle ticks in his jaw. "Why don't you?"

"Because…" I try to gather my scattered thoughts, which seems to be a regular thing for me lately. I'm nowhere near as poised or collected as I used to be, and I'd like to blame it on him, but he's only part of the equation. "In my experience, trust gets broken."

"I won't do that." He holds my gaze, unwavering. "I'm not afraid to put in the hard yards until you believe me." His smirk becomes cocky. "Besides, you can't lump me in with that other asshole. I'm not him."

He's right. He's not. He's more dangerous. Because I'm out of control around him. But then, I'm also tough. Really, it boils down to one thing: do I trust myself to survive whatever comes my way?

The answer is a resounding yes. I can survive anything. So I nod, and take his hand, and let him lead me to his room.

## Chapter Fifteen

*Devon*

The rest of the week is a cycle of awesomeness. True to her word, Harley doesn't try to push me away again, and while she maintains clear boundaries at the gym, she seems to have worked out how to avoid raising Seth's suspicions at home. When I ask about it, she just says she's given him the impression she's staying with a friend she met in Thailand. Another lie that weighs on my soul. But despite the deception, she and I grow closer, and when I'm with her, I can be completely myself. She doesn't care if I need to stay at the gym later to perfect a kick or do a few more reps on the weights and likewise, I'm happy to hit a bag while she practices grappling with Jase. He and Seth are her main training partners, although she and I spar sometimes. On the whole, we've decided it's best not to grapple since rolling around on the floor gets us a little too excited.

She has a playful nature that's beginning to shine through now she's letting her guard down, and I love it. She's competitive too. When we playfight in my apartment, she hates to lose. She pouts and grumps until I bring her around by worshiping her body the way I know she likes it.

On Friday, we're lying on the sofa—me on the bottom, her on top, her cheek resting on my chest—when I take the plunge and do something I've been building the courage for all day.

"We've got something really good going here, don't we?" I ask.

"Mmhmm," she murmurs in agreement, her fingers toying with the collar of my shirt.

I pause. Now comes the hard part. I hate to pop the peaceful bubble around us, but it needs to happen. My self-respect won't allow the lies—even lies by omission—to continue any longer. "Just think how much better it could be if we didn't have to sneak around."

She stiffens, and her chin tilts up, her hazel eyes locking on mine. "You want to tell people?"

"Well, yeah." I smooth her hair back off her face, fingers trailing along her sharp cheekbones. "We're good together, and the past week has been so nice—better than nice, actually. The best damn week of my life. But I don't want to hide anymore. I hate having to treat you like any other training buddy... Do you trust me enough to go public?"

"Dev—"

"Imagine it," I continue, unwilling to let her complete the thought. "We could spend time together in places other than my apartment. Eat out. Do activities like a normal couple. You wouldn't need to constantly be on edge about Seth finding out." It sounds like bliss to me, so I can only hope it sounds half as appealing to her. After what happened in Thailand, I understand her reluctance, but I'm also afraid that the longer she holds back, the harder it will be to come clean. Maybe she won't ever want to. It's possible that her fear will prevent us from being as good together as I know we can be. Surely I've proven myself by now.

"I suppose so," she mumbles, burying her face in my chest. From the tension in her shoulders, I can tell she has more to say and I wait, not rushing her. Finally, she draws back far enough to look at me. "Emotionally, I'm ready, but we need to ease into it. I'm still too raw to just rip off the band aid."

"Okay." I have her agreement, and joy bubbles up within me. I kiss the top of her head. "Thank you, baby. This means a lot to me."

She smiles tentatively. "I know. You're okay with taking it slow?"

I nod. "The sooner the better as far as I'm concerned, but as long as I know for sure it's happening, we don't have to tell everyone at once." I laugh, seeing her surprise. "We're on the right track. I don't mind waiting for a couple of days to do it properly."

"All right."

I breathe a sigh of relief, a weight lifting from my shoulders. Having the matter resolved between us makes me feel better about the future. Optimistic.

Fingers crossed it works out.

---

*DEVON*

The next day, we take the plunge with our first public outing, a hike up the Las Vegas Overlook Trail. Apparently she's never done it before and it's something we can do together without being scrutinized by everyone we know. To me, it feels like progress. It's not quite where I'd like us to be, but it's a step in the right direction.

Before we leave, I dress in shorts and a t-shirt, and slather on sunscreen. The sun beats down outside and only a few fluffy white clouds float across the sky. Harley wears a tank top that reveals miles of tanned skin and lean muscle. Coming up behind her, I skim my palms along her upper arms. She shivers and leans back onto my chest.

"Thank you for this," I whisper.

She smiles up at me, and I'm definitely not imagining the affection in her eyes. "See if you want to thank me by the time we get back."

"I will." My lips graze over her temple and down to her mouth. She sighs, opening to me, and her body grows languid in my arms. My dick perks up, so I stop before I decide I'd rather stay here and get naked.

"Come on." I twine my fingers between hers. "Let's get going."

"Just wait for me to get my shoes."

She grabs her runners and we drive out to the start of the trail. I've done it a few times before, but I try to see it from a fresh perspective. The vegetation is scrubby, with nothing dense enough to cast shade, and the ground is dry and rocky. All in all, the desert around Vegas isn't pretty or welcoming, but it is beautiful in a barren and ruthless way.

We start walking. The trail slopes steeply in places but our breathing remains steady. I watch Harley's ponytail skim over her back as it sways side to side with each step. I let her take the lead, and it feels very much like a metaphor for my life right now.

If only every day could be like this one. The sun warms my back and except for voices in front of us, all I can hear is the crunching of our shoes on the ground and my own breathing. It's perfect. I've missed the quiet. The outdoors. And, if I'm honest, Devon's presence is also contributing to my good mood. We've hardly spoken, but he's a reassuring figure at my back. Every time I look around, he's smiling—and I don't mean a casual "this is cool" smile, he's full-on beaming like he's having the time of his life, which makes me feel the same because he isn't bored with me. He seems content to be here with me. Before this week, I'd never have guessed he was so easy to please, but I've made a lot of assumptions that haven't turned out to be accurate, and honestly, I'm ashamed of myself for that.

"Do you go hiking often?" I ask over my shoulder, inhaling a lungful of fresh air. It doesn't have the same texture as it does in Thailand, but it's still better than what you get in the city. I grew up in a little town where both the air and night sky were clear, and sometimes I miss it.

"Every now and then," he replies. "It's not a regular thing."

A smile teases at the corners of my mouth. I like that we're doing something special together. "Have you done any overnight trips?"

"Yeah." His tone is casual. "The boys and I go camping once a year. Get away from our lives for a while, you know."

It surprises me that he needs to get away from anything. He seems to take it all in stride. In contrast, I'm a hot mess.

"Where do you go?"

"Out of state, usually. Jase likes Colorado. Gabe prefers Cali."

"And you?"

"Anywhere we go, it's a new adventure, so I don't really care."

"You're full of surprises, Green."

He snorts. "And you're not?"

I pivot, hands on my hips, and cock a brow. "What's that supposed to mean?"

One of his shoulders hitches up, then falls. "You're a badass muay thai princess who likes to cook, and sleep-talks in another language. Your glare could freeze a man's balls off, but secretly, you're a snuggler. You act as if you don't give a shit about anything, but I think you feel so deeply that you prefer not to let anyone in. That way they can't hurt you when they leave. You're a walking contradiction. All surprises."

My throat is drier than the desert warrants. He sees far more of me than I want him to, and it scares the crap out of me. I choose my next words carefully because my brain is screaming at me not to be stupid. To protect myself. To raise the drawbridge and arm the cannons.

"You're more perceptive than you seem, and you're not as... straightforward... as I expected, either."

His teeth flash. "Is that your way of saying you like me?"

"You have your moments." Before he can make any further observations, I spin on my heel and start back up the slope. My sneaker lands on a loose rock and skitters out from under me. I start to plummet toward the ground, but an arm wraps around my waist and catches me. The air whooshes from my lungs and tears spring to my eyes as I gasp for breath.

"Careful." He rubs a hand down my back. "I've got you."

I straighten, but when I expect him to release me, he doesn't. His gaze burns into mine, uncharacteristically serious.

"I mean it, Harls. Whatever happens, I've got you."

Blinking rapidly, I tell myself it's a result of being winded and not because of the sudden punch of emotion in my gut.

"I believe you," I whisper, even as the voice in the back of my head screams that I'm a fool whose world is about to implode all over again. Screw the voice. It doesn't control me.

My lips meet his in something that goes beyond a kiss. It's a collision—of our lips, and our hearts, each beating wildly against the other. Our very souls.

Someone coughs behind us and we break apart.

"Sorry to interrupt," a woman says, her cheeks red as she looks anywhere except at us. She and her companion, an older guy with hiking poles, stand behind us, their path clearly blocked. His gaze is fixed on Devon.

"Say, are you that MMA fighter?" He seems to rack his mind for a name. "Devon Green." He holds up a finger. "*Dangerous* Devon Green."

Devon's face lights up. "I am indeed. This is my girlfriend, Harley Isles."

It's the first time we've told anyone, and electricity zaps across my skin, shocking me with how much I like it.

"Do you mind if we get a photo?" the guy asks, digging his cell phone from his pocket.

"Not at all."

The woman takes it from him, and I step aside,

certain he doesn't want me in the shot since Devon is the one who's famous, but he gestures for me to stand on his other side. I hesitate, knowing there's a chance this photo could end up all over social media by nightfall. Seth might see it. But then I straighten my back and join them. Seth is my family, but Devon means more to me with each passing day, and he needs this. Needs to know I'm willing to stand beside him. That I'm proud to be with him.

The corners of his eyes crinkle as the lady snaps the pictures, and then we break apart so the man can check them.

"Thanks so much," he says, pumping Devon's hand and then smiling at me. "You've made my day." He glances at his companion. "We'll leave you in peace now." He winks knowingly. "Enjoy yourselves, but not too much."

"Oh, we will," Devon assures him, and I snort-laugh at the barely concealed innuendo.

The couple continue, and Devon and I exchange a look. My cheeks are flushed from being caught making out with a boy in a public place. I can't help but flashback to when I was fifteen and Mom turned on the porch light just as Peter Sutton and I were getting to second base. *Cringe.*

On the other hand, Devon is eyeing me in a way that suggests all kind of activities not appropriate for the location.

I gesture toward the trail. "We should probably…"

"Yeah." He rakes his fingers through his hair. "Save the other stuff for later." He offers me his other hand, and I intertwine my fingers with his. "Let's go, girlfriend."

The rest of the day is a blur of small talk and camaraderie. Devon is good company, and when we return to the city, I can't help feeling disappointed that our afternoon has come to an end. Strangely, I'm looking forward to telling our friends about us because it means we can have more days like this one, and that sounds pretty perfect. As long as Seth doesn't rip the ground out from under me.

# Chapter Sixteen

*Devon*

"Hey, Dev, you got a minute?" Seth calls as I enter the gym on Monday morning.

My stomach clenches, my instincts screaming that he's seen the photo that guy from yesterday posted online and has learned the truth about Harley and me before we had a chance to break the news gently. But then he throws me a relaxed smile and my heart starts beating again. It's on the tip of my tongue to blurt out the truth and get it off my chest, but I promised Harley I'd let her speak to him first.

"Got some good news," he says.

"What's that?" I should be relieved but there's this slimy sensation in the pit of my gut that hates maintaining the charade for even a minute longer.

"You've been offered a fight on the Nightshade card."

"Really?" Excitement kicks away the guilt. The Nightshade event is where Harley will have her eight-woman eliminator tournament, which means I get to fight on the same night as my girl. We can train together, and kick ass together. It's only six or so weeks away but I'm down for it, like always. "That's awesome. Against who?"

He flashes teeth. "Karson Hayes."

I fist pump.

He smirks. "Knew you'd like that."

"Fuck yeah, I do."

Karson Hayes is an all-round douche. I've fought him before and lost, but you can bet your ass I'm going to take him down this time. I have to. As if I'd let a girl-hitting jerk beat me.

"Did his opponent pull out? I heard he'd already been matched for the event."

"He got injured during training. The promoter asked around for a fill-in and I put your name in the hat." Seth holds out a fist and I bump his knuckles with mine. "You got this, Dev. You've come a long way since last time; you're unconventional as hell but that's part of what makes you such a good fighter. Just keep training like you are, and he won't have a shot."

"Thanks, man." Forget the masculine fist bump. I go in for a one-armed hug, ignoring his groan of protest. It's been a while since I had a fight. Not for any particular reason, that's just the way it's worked out, and I'm psyched to get back in the cage. It's one of my favorite places. When I match my body and wits against another guy in such a raw way, I'm truly alive.

Seth pulls away and shrugs a shoulder. "You earned it. I know you'll do me proud."

"Count on it." I'm buzzing. Already, I can't wait to hear my song play over the speakers to signal it's my time to strut my stuff all the way to the ring.

"Focus on takedowns today," he says. "Hayes is crap on the ground. You can practice with Jase and Harley."

"Done." Nodding to him, I cross to the skipping ropes. Then, after a quick warm-up, I join Jase and Harley. She's listening intently to whatever he's saying, and his slate gray eyes slide over to me as I approach.

"Heard the news, bro." He offers me a fist to bump. "You'll take him."

"You bet I will." I grin. "Gotta defend Lena's honor."

He rolls his eyes. "I already did that."

"What's going on?" Harley asks, looking from me to Jase and back again, her attention lingering on my chest in a way I like a little too much.

"I've got a fight the same night as you," I tell her. "Against Lena's ex. The guy who cornered you at the Steel Angels event."

"Oh. He was an ass."

"He is," I continue, "but forget that. This means you and I can train together for Nightshade. Coordinate schedules. All that jazz."

She cocks her head. "We train together anyway."

"Yeah, but having something to work toward makes it different." I scan her face, noting her curious expression, and realize belatedly that my excitement isn't only about the next six weeks. I'm thinking of all the times we could do this in future. This could be the beginning of a life together.

*Hang on.*

I'm planning a future. With a woman.

I mean, I knew I was ass over heels crazy about her but I'm not a planner. Spontaneity is my thing. What does it mean that I'm already thinking of the future? Nerves prickle under my skin, making me hyperaware of everything, but my gut says the change is a good thing, and I'm a man who trusts his gut so I go with it.

I turn back to Jase. "I need to practice my takedowns."

He nods. "You and Harley can alternate on each other. She needs to improve hers, too."

Grinning like a fool, I can't help but think of how perfectly suited we are. Now all I need is for her to see it too.

---

*HARLEY*

For the seventh morning in a row, I wake and stare at a ceiling that's not my own and wonder how I ended up here. I never expected to fall into a new relationship when I returned from Thailand, and I'm still figuring out how Devon and I fit together. He called me his girlfriend but I feel like so much more. We haven't actually been on a date, unless you count the Steel Angels or the walk to the lookout, but despite that, we spend most of our free time together, and I wouldn't have it any other way. He's surprisingly thoughtful and funny, and when his arms go around me, I have this lovely fuzzy sensation in my chest that I never expected to experience.

Rolling onto my side, I study him. He's relaxed in sleep and looks vulnerable—not a word I'd ever have associated with him. His nose is in perfect proportion to the rest of his face, and his lashes are long and dark, sweeping over his cheekbones. He sighs, breath easing between his parted lips. Could he and I work long-term?

I consider the question from every angle. Our lifestyles are certainly compatible. We both live to train. I'd previously believed him to be too much of a party animal for me but except for the Steel Angels event, I haven't seen him in any tabloids or heard him mention any parties since we met. He definitely hasn't been living it up over the past week because all of his free time has been spent with me.

Today, I have to tell Seth about us. I'm dreading it. I'm afraid he'll see it as a double betrayal, because while I'm his sister by blood, he considers the guys he coaches to be family too. How will he feel when he discovers that Devon and I have been lying to him? Worse, what will it do to me if I lose him?

Ugh. I need to work off my anxious energy or hit something.

Dragging myself out of bed, I dress in a pair of shorts and a tank top, lace up my runners, let myself out of the apartment, and hit the pavement. Five miles later, my thoughts aren't any clearer. Devon and I eat breakfast together, then I head to the gym while he does his cardio. It's still early and the building is locked, so I use the key Seth had cut for me and spend fifteen minutes taking out my confusion on a punching bag before Seth turns up. The sight of his square-jawed face and familiar blue-green eyes sets off another episode of guilt.

"Morning," he calls as he kicks off his shoes and wanders across the mats. "What'd the bag do to you?"

"Pissed me off." I pause, hands on hips as I catch my breath, watching him watch me and wondering what he sees.

"Take you through some pads soon?" he asks, then cocks his head. "No music and no timer? You must really want to kill someone."

"Something like that."

He heads over to where his gear sits alongside the ring and slips a thigh pad over each leg, a belly pad around his middle, and a Thai pad on one arm. He sets up the timer for five-minute rounds and grabs the other Thai pad. I shake my arms to loosen them as I cross to join him. He holds up a pad.

"Jab."

I jab.

"Hook."

I comply.

"Cross, hook, leg kick."

I do the combo, ending with the thud of my shin into the thigh pad. He continues calling out moves but other than that, we train in silence. Then, in the break between rounds, he sighs and rubs a hand over his reddish-blonde buzz cut.

"So, you've met someone, huh?"

My lungs seize. "What do you mean?"

He exhales, his chest heaving as if he wants to have this conversation as little as I do, and his lips twist wryly. "I'm not an idiot. You've hardly been home, and I doubt you've been spending all of your free time with an old friend. Avoiding me doesn't stop me from wondering where you are. But I figure you'll tell me when you're ready."

He's given me a perfect opportunity to come clean. To tell him everything. Yet I can't help but think of the way his gaze will shutter when I confess to shacking up with one of his fighters. He was basically my dad growing up, and his expression tells me it hurts him that I'm not being open.

I owe him the truth.

I suck in a breath and gather my courage. I can do this.

"It's Devon." My mouth is dry as dust. *Woman-up, Isles.* "I'm dating Devon."

For a moment, his eyes narrow, but then he laughs. "Good one, Harley. You had me going."

"I'm not kidding." My heart is about ready to bust out of my chest. "We're together."

"You're serious?" he demands. "You've been seeing one of my fighters behind my back?"

The ground falls away beneath my feet. I can't unsee the betrayal and pain etched on his face. He gave me a home and a fresh start, and I hurt him in return.

"Seth…" I reach for him and he jerks away. "It just happened. We have feelings for each other, and you can't turn those off. I'm sorry for breaking my promise, but we're good together and if you give us a chance, you'll see that."

His arms fall to his sides, and his eyes are wide with disbelief. "There are lots of decent guys around. Why did you have to go for someone at the gym?"

"Because I care for him." My voice is strong despite the guilt that pierces my heart. He has every right to be unhappy, but I won't deny my feelings. Devon deserves better than that.

"Oh, Harley." He sighs, the sound full of disappointment. My chest aches and I press a hand to my sternum to ease the discomfort. It's like I've breathed in dry ice. I can't stand the way he's looking at me like he doesn't even know who I am. "I can't train both of you. Don't you get that? What if something happens and you break up? Then the drama spills over into the gym and affects everyone else. It's too messy. I've seen it before, and it doesn't work."

Doubt rolls over me like a wave, drenching me from head to toe. Maybe we didn't think this through as much as we should have. Perhaps my brother has a point. But no, I steel myself. I can't write us off like that when we're only just beginning.

"What if it's the best thing that ever happens for

either of us?" I ask. "Don't we deserve to figure that out?"

He drags a padded hand down his face and groans. "Yeah, maybe, but you've put me in a shitty position. I can't train both of you. There's zero room for drama in my gym. One of you has to go, and you're my baby sister..." His eyes gleam with emotion, and he touches my shoulder the same way he used to when he needed to reassure me as a kid. God, I hate how it fills me with warmth and dread at the same time. "I abandoned you once, and left you to fend for yourself. I won't do that again. It has to be him."

Squeezing my eyes shut, I fight the storm of emotions threatening to overwhelm me. My throat is tight and I can hardly speak. Dozens of thoughts fly through my mind. Seth thinks he's doing the right thing, but he can't kick Devon out of the gym. MMA is his life. It would break him. He doesn't deserve that.

A sudden burst of anger heats my gut, and I get up in Seth's face. Never mind that he's twice my size. I know he won't lay a finger on me.

"For fuck's sake, you can't be serious. I won't let you get rid of him because he had the audacity to date me."

His jaw firms. "It's my gym, and the rules are there for a reason."

At that moment, the door swings open and Devon strides in. The grin falls from his face as he catches sight of our expressions. Seth crosses his arms over his chest, glaring at Devon the same way he eyed every guy I ever so much as mentioned during high school—despite the fact I never actually dated any of them. I gulp as a montage of all the knockout punches I've seen him throw plays through my mind in slow motion.

"Do you usually let your girlfriends do the heavy lifting for you?" he snaps across the space.

Devon drops his bag and makes his way toward us. "She wanted to talk to you first." He scans me as though checking I'm all right, then slings his arm around my waist and stands staunchly beside me. "You good, babe?"

I nod. "I was just explaining to Seth why he doesn't need to kick either of us out."

Devon's face blanches. "Come on, man, we're all professionals here. Surely, there's no need for that."

I hate this. Hate the tension between them that never used to exist. I put it there.

"You broke the fucking rules." Seth's voice rises and his nostrils flare. "I warned all of you not to touch my sister."

Devon's arm tightens around me, but I resist the urge to melt into him and let him take care of this mess for me. It's every bit as much my fault as his, if not more. I'm the one who's new here, after all.

"She means everything to me," Devon says.

I glance at him, the words taking me by surprise. "I do?"

He smiles softly. "Yeah, you do."

I turn back in time to see my brother's lips pinch together. He looks like he'd rather be anywhere but here.

"I'm sorry," I tell him. "I didn't mean for this to happen, but you must remember what it feels like to be with someone and have it just click. You and Ashlin were inseparable from the start."

Bad idea. At the mention of his failed marriage, his eyes narrow, his jaw clenches, then he pinches the bridge of his nose and exhales slowly.

"You both need to leave."

Shit. This just got real. "But—"

"No buts." He gestures at the exit. "I need to think, and you need to give me space to get my head around this. In the meantime, figure out if whatever this is"—he waves his hand back and forth between us—"is worth losing your place here."

I want to argue, but I can tell from the set of his jaw that he isn't willing to hear it, so Devon and I collect our things and leave, because we don't really have a choice.

But he'll calm down and come around. Won't he?

# Chapter Seventeen

*Devon*

Holy fuck. My life just imploded.

After Harley and I step outside, I stare at the door for far too long before moving, then pull Harley into my arms and hold her close.

"I'm so sorry. I didn't think he'd react that way." I kiss the top of her head and try not to freak out as I think through the implications. If Seth is serious and one of us has to leave the gym—most likely me—does that mean I won't see my friends anymore? Will they be forced to choose sides? And can I still compete in the fight he lined up for me, or will that opportunity be lost?

I put those worries to the back of my mind. They don't matter in the grand scheme of things. What's more important is the fact that I'd been sure our coming clean wouldn't be as big a deal as Harley feared. But I was wrong. Seth is really upset.

Have I driven a wedge between them? Cut her off from her sole source of stability during a turbulent time in her life? Damn, I hope not. I need to make sure my girl is okay.

"How are you doing?" I ask gently.

Her shoulders hunch. "I want to say I wasn't expecting it, but he's always been stubborn when he has an idea in his head about how things should be." She straightens, and her hands fall away from her face. Her expression is so weary it tears at my soul. "I just wish he'd give us a chance to show we can train together and be together without everything going up in flames." She shakes her head, and her eyes shine with tears. "I'm so sorry. I know how much you love the gym, and everything was fine until I came along."

"Don't be." I grip her by the shoulders and stare down at her, willing her to see the truth in my eyes. The depth of my feelings for her. Much as I hate the rift forming between Seth and me, and I haven't wrapped my head around what it would mean to lose the gym—my place to belong—I know, beyond a doubt, that I will survive it. I'm not sure my heart can live through the loss of Harley.

"There are other gyms." I lean forward to kiss her but stop short when I see her wariness. "There's only one Harley Isles, and I'm not prepared to give her up yet."

Her chin juts mutinously. "I know how much Crown MMA means to you."

"But do you know what *you* mean to me?" I can't help it if I sound exasperated. I am. "You're more important than the gym is. It's just a place."

"Really?" I can tell she wants to believe me.

"Yes. My main concern is you and Seth. I have a support system. Friends and family. He's all you've got, and I know how important he is to you. What if this damages your relationship?" I'll never forgive myself if their bond is weakened because of me.

She pales. "We'll be okay." Her voice shakes. "I mean, we managed to get through eight years of me being overseas, so this can't break us, right?"

"I don't know, Harls." I wish I did, so I could reassure her.

"At least I'm starting to make new friends," she says, as much to herself as to me. "Meet other people."

My stomach roils. "Do you mean Sydney and Lena?"

Because if so, there's a chance she'll lose them too, if Jase and Gabe decide to take Seth's side since they warned me not to screw things up and I did anyway. Then who would she have left? Just me? While I'll happily be everything to her that I can, I don't want her to feel isolated and alone.

She winces. "You think they'll take a step back when they find out?"

"I'd like to think not, but I don't know. Lena is stubborn, and Sydney has a massive heart, so they might ignore the drama, but it's definitely possible, out of loyalty to their guys."

Her face falls, and I hate it. But then she seems to muster her strength. "No. I refuse to dwell on the worst case scenario. We need to come up with a plan."

I hesitate, unsure whether I should mention what's on my mind.

"What is it?" she asks, frowning.

"Maybe..." I fill my lungs with air and say the last thing I want to. "Maybe we should put a pause on things between us. Then I can find another gym, and you can repair your relationship with Seth."

Her lips part, and her eyes widen with shock. "Are you breaking up with me?"

"No!" I drop my hands from her shoulders and try to scoop her into a hug, but she squirms and I'm forced to release her. "But if we don't see each other for a couple of weeks, and give Seth time to adjust to the idea of us without being in his face about it then he might be more willing to accept us together long-term." I cup her face in my palms. "I don't want to come between you and your brother."

She shakes her head vehemently. "I won't do that. We've finally put ourselves out there. I'm not stuffing us back into a closet for the sake of smoothing things over with Seth a little faster." She tugs on her ponytail, teeth embedded in her lip while she thinks. "Here's what we'll do. We'll give Seth a few hours to mull it over, and I'll talk to him again tonight."

"We both will," I counter.

She presses her lips together and hesitates, clearly not sold on the idea, but if she wants to stay together and damn the consequences, then that starts now.

"We need to present a united front," I add.

She inclines her head. "Okay, maybe you've got a point."

"Damn right I do." A car turns into the parking lot, and we both glance over to see who it is. Fortunately, not someone either of us know well.

"If someone does have to leave, it should be me." She exhales raggedly. "You've been here for years, and I'm new. You'd have stayed here for years more if I hadn't come along."

I can tell she's beating herself up, and I won't have it. "Harls, no. I'll go. You're Seth's sister, and he has all those grand plans about making a splash on the women's circuit. Don't worry about me. Whatever happens, I'll be fine."

She looks dubious. "We'll talk about it later."

"So, what now?"

She considers this for a moment. "There's someone I need to talk to. I'll give her a call and see if she's free. Then perhaps I could come by your place."

I don't want to separate from her. My instincts shout at me that it's the wrong thing to do, but logically I know her plan is sound. I kiss her lips, lingering for a few seconds to breathe her in as though it's the last time we might ever do this.

"We can sit in my car while you make that call."

---

*Harley*

There's only one person who's ever been able to manage Seth when he's in a mood, and that's his ex-wife, Ashlin. I follow Devon to his car and climb into the passenger seat, then scroll my contacts until I find her details. I know Ashlin is unlikely to speak to Seth on my behalf. As far as I'm aware, they haven't been in touch since they divorced three years ago, but I'm hoping she can give me some pointers.

I swipe the call icon, and reach across to take Devon's hand, needing the physical contact to anchor me. The call connects, and I cross my fingers she'll have time to talk.

"Hey, Ash."

"Hi Harley, how are you?" Her voice is strong but sweet, exactly like I remember.

"Um, mostly good, but I have a problem. How about you? We haven't talked for ages."

"It's been too long. Is there something I can help with? I'd love to see your beautiful face in person."

"Yes," I exclaim, overcome with relief. "Maybe we could meet today? I need your help."

"Absolutely." Something rustles in the background. "We could get coffee. Maybe around three this afternoon if that works?"

"That would be perfect." God, I'm so glad she's my friend.

"Great! I'll choose a café that Seth isn't likely to visit so we can talk without an inquisition."

I cringe, hating the thought that Ashlin chooses to hide from the man who used to adore her. I also hate feeling like I'm betraying Seth a second time by seeing her. It isn't as though I've lied to him about our friendship. He just hasn't asked and I haven't volunteered the information.

One of Devon's brows hitches up questioningly.

"I'll text you a place," she says. "Have to get back to work now."

"See you then."

"Bye, Harley."

Ending the call, I offer Devon a smile. "I'm going to see her later today."

He raises our joint hands to his mouth and kisses mine. "Who is it?"

"A friend."

"Oh?" His nose crinkles. "Now I'm intrigued. I need the details, Harls."

I sigh. "Seth's ex, Ashlin."

His eyes widen. "His ex-wife?"

"That's the one."

"Wow." He exhales slowly, clearly distracted from our current situation. "Do you keep in contact with her?" He holds up a finger. "Wait, you obviously do. What's she like? I always wondered what kind of woman Seth married. I've seen photos because I googled him when I first joined the gym, but I never heard what happened. Why'd they separate?"

"Honestly?" I shrug. "I don't know. I've asked, and neither of them have said much about it."

"But if you had to guess?"

Shaking my head, I don't answer. "I care about them both, and they've shared things with me in confidence, so I'm not going to guess. It's up to them if they want to tell people what happened, and clearly they don't."

I have my suspicions though. I'm not sure what the catalyst was, but my guess is that Seth let Ashlin down somehow or messed up. She's the steadiest, most consistently open-hearted person I know and I can't imagine why else she'd end things with him when neither of them have truly recovered from it.

"You're a good person," he says, even if he looks disappointed not to get the gossip. "Trustworthy. I love that about you."

My discomfort must show on my face because he sighs. "It will be okay. Seth will see reason. After all, we've got a secret weapon now. Just make me a promise?"

"What?"

"Come back to me." Vulnerability steals over his face. "Even if you talk with Ashlin and decide that my idea of separating temporarily is the best way to go, promise it won't be permanent. I need you in my life."

Leaning over the space between the seats, I kiss him. "I promise."

## Chapter Eighteen

*HARLEY*

A few hours later, I walk to the café where Ashlin chose to meet. As I enter, I scan the tables and catch sight of her in the corner. The place is dimly lit with wood surfaces everywhere. She stands, and I take stock of her. It's been eight years since I saw her in person, and although we've had a few video calls, seeing her on a camera is nothing like laying eyes on her in real life. She's as petite as ever—barely more than five feet tall, with a slight build and sleek brunette hair that's cut in a long bob. Back when I saw her regularly, she had beachy waves that cascaded over her back and shoulders. She smiles as she comes around the table toward me and the corners of her eyes crinkle. Her cheeks are more angular than they used to be, but I guess that's the effect of age. She was twenty-two when I moved away—four years older than me and eight years younger than Seth—but she's thirty now, and more stunning than ever. It's always amazed me that someone as feminine and popular as her would want to be friends with a short-tempered tomboy like me, but she never seemed to notice the difference between us.

"Harley, it's so good to see you!" She envelops me in a floral-scented hug, and I close my arms around her, taking care not to squeeze too hard in case I break her. But I ought to remember that Ashlin has always been tougher than she looks, and she squeezes me back tight enough to wind me.

"You look good, Ash." I pull back and re-familiarize myself with her features. Eyes a shade browner than mine. Pointed chin. Pixie-like and delicate. "I've missed you."

"Same goes," she agrees, her lips lifting into a ready smile. That hasn't changed, either. Ashlin has a smile for every occasion. "I thought about visiting you in Thailand but didn't want to interfere with your training." She gestures for me to sit, and I do, while she returns to her place on the other side. "What brought you home?"

"You mean to Vegas?" I ask wryly. "Cedar Bend is home."

She inclines her head. "True. So?"

With as few words as possible, I tell her about Thaklaew and the fight I was supposed to lose. She hums sympathetically, reaches across the table and touches my hand.

"I'm sorry. That must have been rough. Did you love him?"

Glancing at the surface of the table, I raise one shoulder and then drop it. "I don't think so. It was just... convenient. Dependable."

Her lips twitch. "How romantic."

Despite myself, I grin. "Have you ever known me to be the romantic type?"

"I live in hope."

157

An image of Devon flashes into my mind. Her hope isn't entirely unfounded.

Her eyes narrow. "What was that?"

"What was what?" I ask stupidly.

"Harley Isles," she exclaims. "You were thinking of a boy. Don't try to deny it, I know that look. Wait, is that why you need advice?"

Holding my palms up, I concede the point. She's always been good at reading people. It's part of what makes her such a good teacher. "Yeah, okay. There's someone new, and we've landed in a bit of a sticky situation."

"Who is it?" She waves a waiter over and orders a fresh coffee. I ask for one of my own.

Butterflies winging around my stomach, I lean onto my forearms and lower my voice. "Is it going to bother you to talk about Seth?"

She gazes at me thoughtfully. "No, but I'm curious what he has to do with it. Does he disapprove?"

I pause, trying to figure out how to phrase this. Ashlin is the closest thing to a best friend I've ever had, and I don't want her to think poorly of me for jumping straight from a relationship with one man on the professional fighting scene to another. "I'm seeing Devon Green."

One perfectly arched brow shoots up. "As in, 'Dangerous' Devon Green? The guy Seth trains?"

I nod to confirm. "Yeah, that's him."

"Ah." Her tone says she understands, but then she adds, "I've seen photos of him. He's hot."

"Fun, too. And sweet."

She mimics my pose, leaning toward me on her elbows. "Seth doesn't like you dating one of his guys."

"No," I admit. "He specifically asked me not to."

"Oh, Harley."

"We told him this morning, and he basically said one of us had to leave the gym because he won't train us both. He thinks it'll get too messy if we break up."

She winces. "He has a point."

"I know." Ducking my head, I do my best to ignore the logic because I don't want to think about me and Devon breaking up. "I don't think that will happen though. Devon is… well, he's special."

She tilts her head and studies me. "He must be, for you to risk falling out with Seth over him." She purses her lips. "He's probably just as married to the sport as Seth is."

"Fine by me. Remember, I lived at a gym for eight years."

"So you did." The crinkles around her eyes deepen. "Perhaps it's a match made in heaven. Except for the whole ultimatum thing. Do you love him?"

"I don't know." I shrug helplessly. "How are you supposed to figure stuff like that out?"

"Well…" She holds my gaze, searching for something in it, but I'm not sure what. "If you can't picture the future without him, and the thought of losing him makes you want to cry, then it's probably love."

I consider this. The fact is, I do tend to imagine him when I think of the future these days, and the idea of him getting tired of my hang-ups and leaving makes my chest tight. Do I want to cry? No, not really. But then, I don't often cry. It's not the way I cope with things. Ashlin, on the other hand, is far more emotionally driven than me.

"Thanks, Ash. Is that how you—" I bite my tongue. It's none of my business how she felt about Seth, or whether she still thinks of him. Yeah, maybe I loved having her as my sister but that doesn't give me the right to poke into her life.

Her expression softens. "Yeah. But on a different note, what is it you want my help with?"

"Figuring out how to talk Seth around."

The waitress arrives with our coffees, and I wrap my hands around mine, warming my fingers, which are colder than usual.

"That's not going to be easy." She blows on the surface of her drink, then sips it. "You know how stubborn he is once he makes a decision."

I do, but that doesn't mean I can't hope for something better. "Any suggestions?"

She shrugs. "It's been years since I saw him. He could have changed since then."

I snort. "Doubt it. He's like an immovable object. Everything changes around him, but he stays the same."

She smiles softly, something a little wistful in her expression. "He's not a bad guy. He just has a certain view of the world, and he prefers not to talk about awkward topics if he can avoid it."

"I know." Despite our difficulties, I love him. He always filled the role of my protector and I suppose it's hard to ask him to drop it now.

"Hmm." Ashlin ponders my question. "Honestly, the best thing you can do is show him you're serious with your actions. Stay strong together and prove that you're in it for the long haul. If he sees you as a solid unit, his perception of the risk will decrease. At the moment, you're a big unknown for him." She reaches over and pats my hand sympathetically. "You're going to have to be patient, honey."

I deflate. That wasn't the answer I'd wanted. I'd hoped she could give me a quick fix I could implement tonight and have everything mostly back to normal tomorrow. "Do you think it's worth talking to him?"

"Unless you lose your temper, it probably won't make things worse." She gives me a look. "Are you likely to get angry with him?"

"Uh, maybe."

She nods, as though she expected this. "I know it's not what you want to hear, but just go along with him for now. Show him you're two adults in a mature relationship and that you can handle whatever comes your way. He'll change his mind eventually."

"You think?"

Her lips curve up. "I do. But I'll tell you what might soften him up."

"What?" I lean forward, eager to hear more.

"Buy him a growler of red ale from the Bulldog Brewery." She winks. "It's his favorite."

My heart lifts. "Thanks, Ash."

Despite her advice not being what I'd hoped, I feel more optimistic than I did earlier.

"No problem. Happy to help. And hey, now that you're in the city, we can see each other regularly. Actually," she wets her lips with her tongue, "I thought I might come to those fights you have in a few weeks. I've watched you on YouTube, but I want to see how far you've come in person." Her eyes are bright with moisture. "I'm so proud of you."

My throat constricts. "I'd love for you to come."

She tucks a strand of dark hair behind her ear. "I might not be able to talk to you at the time, but I'll text you after, and I'll be there for you."

I scoot around the table and give her a hug, blinking back tears of my own. "Thanks. You're the best."

I back off before I get overly emotional. The rest of our visit passes too quickly. When she drops me off at Devon's, I wish I could invite her in to visit for longer, but I have other things that need attending to, so with a heart heavier than I'd like, I say goodbye with a promise to meet again soon.

---

*DEVON*

Harley and I decide to follow Ashlin's suggestion. Much as I can tell the inaction bothers her, and she'd rather go kick down Seth's door and demand he rethink his decision, instead we pick up a growler of red ale from the Bulldog Brewery, and drop by his place.

We knock on the condo door rather than letting ourselves in with Harley's key.

When Seth opens the door, a scowl on his face, I thrust the growler into his arms. He steps back, stunned, and glances down at it.

"What's this?"

"A gift."

His scowl slips for a moment. "Uh, thanks. How'd you know it's my favorite?"

I tap the side of my nose. "I pay attention."

"Right." His expression is dubious. "Have you guys thought about what you want to do?"

"Yes." Harley nods and links her arm with mine. "I'll keep training at Crown MMA, and Devon will explore other options." She gives me a look that says she's not completely happy with the plan.

"Well." I can tell he's taken aback. "Okay. If you're sure that's what you want."

"It is," I say firmly.

He nods, and it's almost respectful. "Did you want to come in?"

"Not tonight." Harley and I discussed this previously and decided it was best not to push our luck by flaunting our relationship so soon after coming clean.

He holds up the growler. "Thanks for stopping by. I appreciate it." He sighs, and looks from Harley to me, and back again. "I hope you know what you're doing."

We say goodbye and head away. I can't help but hope that this is a temporary measure. That he'll realize we can be both romantic and training partners, but I have a feeling it will take him a while to come around to our way of seeing things—if he does at all.

On the way back to my place, I glance over at Harley.

"What should we do if he doesn't change his mind?"

She stares at her reflection in the window. "He will."

"But if he doesn't."

She turns to me. "Not an option."

I shake my head. She clearly doesn't want to talk about it, but I'm not sure that being an ostrich is the best way to go. If we don't deal with this now, she might resent me a few months down the road because of what she's sacrificed to be with me. Still, I let it go. We can talk about it tomorrow.

I WAKE THE FOLLOWING DAY WITH A COMPLICATED knot of emotions in my gut. Grief, for the potential loss of my friendship with Seth and my home at Crown MMA, worry for what Harley stands to lose, and a sense of lingering uncertainty about the future. While I lie in bed, I think of Seth. In some ways, I understand where he's coming from. Interpersonal relationships in what's effectively a place of work are messy, and I haven't always been the type of guy you'd want to hook up with your baby sister. I've never wanted to settle down until now. But this is different, and I need to prove that to him.

I wake Harley with a kiss and help get her out the door, stopping to hug her before she leaves.

"Come back to me soon," I murmur against her hair.

"I will," she promises.

When she's gone, I sit in bed and call around the other gyms in the area. I find plenty that are willing to offer me a place to train, but none who want to corner the fight that Seth arranged for me against Karson Hayes. My ex-coach has a lot of respect in the community and no one wants to do anything that might offend him.

Asking Gabe or Jase isn't an option. I won't put them in the awkward position of choosing between me and Seth. I don't think it would work in my favor anyway because they both warned me not to mess with Harley.

By lunchtime, I've arranged to train later in the day at Alpha MMA—the gym run by Leo Delaney's father, Grant. For some reason, Leo himself doesn't train there. He and Grant are estranged, although the cause of the estrangement is one of the best-kept secrets in the UFC. Whatever the case, I'm grateful to Alpha MMA for providing a space for me.

While I'm there, the fighters steer clear of me. I do my own thing, and they do theirs. It's a lonely experience though, and I'm worried that I'll slide backward without a good training buddy.

## Chapter Nineteen

*Devon*

Later that evening, I'm well and truly deflated. There's a knock on my door, and I open it to find Harley hovering in the corridor, wearing an expression that's one part hesitation and two parts stubbornness. With her hair in a high ponytail, exposing sharp cheekbones and a strong chin, she's absolutely gorgeous, and longing fills my heart—longing to grab her and kiss her.

"I heard that you couldn't find a corner for Nightshade."

"Not yet," I reply, unsure where this conversation is heading.

She pulls at the end of her ponytail the way I've noticed she does when she's anxious. Need clenches in my gut. Even though we were together last night, it's feels like eons since I touched her. Slowly, I extend a hand and brush my knuckles over her cheek. Her eyes flutter shut and she leans into the caress for a brief moment, but then she's back to business.

"I'll do it."

My pulse ratchets up, hammering so loudly in my ears that I struggle to believe what she's just said. She's willing to do that for me? She must know that it would put even more stress on her relationship with her brother. Does it make me a bad person that joy fizzes through my body, bubbling up in the vicinity of my heart, at the evidence of how much she cares for me?

"Are you sure?" I ask. "I mean, that would be amazing, but what about Seth?"

She shakes her head, the tips of her ponytail brushing her shoulders. "Don't worry about him. It'll work out. You're making a huge sacrifice for me, and I couldn't live with myself if you lost the fight when I'm capable of helping. I've got your back, Dev."

Taking her hands, I step closer, aligning my body with hers. Her warmth permeates the sliver of air between us, tempting me to close the space. "You're amazing. Thank you."

She blinks, then shakes her head as though trying to clear it. "I'm going to get you back in with Seth too."

My brow furrows. "If it happens, it happens. Don't worry about it too much."

Her jaw drops. "But—"

I cut her off. "No buts. I'd rather have you than membership at one particular gym."

Her expression crumples, and then she's kissing me. Our lips collide and I smash that space between us to smithereens. Heat curls through me, slow and sweet, like warm honey, but then I taste salt and pull back. Her cheeks are streaked with tears. Everything inside me stills. I yank her tight to my chest and cradle her head.

"I don't want to be responsible for you losing your fight family," she mutters, voice thick with emotion.

I press my lips to the top of her head. "Baby, you're my family now. And I hope I'm yours too." Although that doesn't allay all of my guilt.

Gently, she disengages, then wipes her cheeks on the hem of her tank top. "I don't know what I did to deserve you." She visibly pulls herself together. "How about we get through the next few weeks and figure out what comes next after Nightshade?"

"Sounds perfect." I intend to have her in my arms every night. "One other thing: no more secrets. From each other, or anyone else. Deal?"

"Deal."

I grin. "So, want to come to dinner with my parents this week?"

She huffs a laugh. "Go big or go home, right?"

---

*Devon*

We're due at my parent's place soon and I've spent the past twenty minutes trying to soothe Harley, who's quietly freaking out. After her bravado a few days ago, she seems to have grown steadily more anxious.

"It's not that big of a big deal," I assure her. "They'll love you." Okay, it kinda is a big deal. I've never brought a girl home for dinner. But laying that out there isn't going to make her feel better.

"Meeting the parents is always a big deal." Her tone makes it clear this ought to be obvious, and I can't help but wonder how many parents she's met in her time. I assume she didn't get to that stage with her ex-coach because surely she would have mentioned it, but how many boys came before? Was she a heart-breaker during high school? God, I wish I knew. I'm hungry for information about her. "What if I say the wrong thing? I sometimes blurt stupid stuff when I'm nervous."

"You'll be okay." I smooth my hands down her arms and smile reassuringly. "My dad is super chill."

She cocks a brow. "And your mom?"

"Less chill," I admit. My arms encircle her waist, holding her close. I can't seem to go for long without touching her. As soon as we're alone, I'm all over her. She doesn't seem to mind. Although she's not the gushy type, she likes physical contact and being close to me.

"Hmm."

My lips drift over her neck and she angles her head to give me better access, then I lift her off my lap and set her on her feet. "Time to go."

"Hang on," she says. "I need to change my outfit."

I snort. "You'll be fine. Mom is gonna love you."

Harley could turn up in a sack and Mom would throw a party. It's the first time I've come close to living life the way she'd like me to.

"No." She digs in her heels. "At least let me put on lip gloss and a different shirt."

I wait while she strides to my room, where she's taken to storing some of her belongings, and returns a few moments later in a white blouse with a pink sheen over her lips.

She gives me a thumbs up. "Good to go."

"Great." I sling a jacket over my arm and escort her to the door, locking it behind us.

Soon after, we arrive at my parents' place.

"Are you sure I won't be intruding?" Harley asks as I knock, gnawing on her lower lip.

I ease my thumb across her mouth, forcing her to stop abusing the soft skin. "I'm certain." Holding a hand up, I add, "And before you mention it, Mom will have plenty of food. She cooks enough to feed an army." I've given her the heads up that I'll be bringing a friend, but didn't say who because I want the pleasure of seeing the shock and joy on her face when she realizes I've finally brought a woman home.

"Ah, her famous roast."

I wink. "Exactly."

Mom pulls the door open and stops short. Her mouth gapes, then closes. She blinks a few times. I grin. No matter what I said about being interested in someone, I doubt she actually expected it to go anywhere. Once she realizes what's happening, she'll be ecstatic, and it's nice to surprise her in a good way for once.

"Mom?" I prompt. "Are you okay?"

"Better than okay." She eyes Harley like the woman is a damn unicorn. I mean, she kinda is, but Mom doesn't know that. "Why don't you introduce me to your lovely friend?"

That's more like it. I wave a hand from one of them to the other. "Mom, this is Harley Isles, my girlfriend. Harls, this is my Mom, Rochelle."

Harley extends a hand. "Nice to meet you, Mrs. Green."

Mom raises trembling fingers to her lips, eyes shining with emotion and—are they tears? She needs to pull herself together before she freaks Harley out more than she already is. Then, all of a sudden, Mom seizes Harley's hand and yanks her into a hug with a lot of force for someone the size of a pixie.

"Just look at you. You're a blessing. The answer to my many, *many* prayers." Releasing Harley—except for an iron grip on her shoulders—she steps back. "Welcome. Please, come in."

I can see Harley having second thoughts, and the

look she sends me the instant Mom turns to search for Pops is on the verge of panic.

"You have a beautiful home," she says, nevertheless, as we enter the living area. "I hope I'm not putting you out by turning up like this."

"Not at all!" Mom's eyeballs threaten to pop out of her head as she whirls around wearing a smile that terrifies me. "We couldn't be more pleased to have you here. Dev's never brought a girl to visit us before. I'd almost given up on him." Her expression softens. "You must be something special."

She is. And while Harley is clearly taken aback by Mom's enthusiastic response, it's also obvious that Mom is growing on her. The woman drives me crazy at times, but people do seem to find her endearing.

"Very special," I agree out loud, pleased when Harley's cheeks flush.

"Jamal!" Mom raises her voice loud enough to be heard from the street. "Devon's new girlfriend is here!"

A few moments later—long enough to show that he won't be bossed around—Pops appears in the doorway, where he pauses to study Harley. He takes her measure in a few seconds.

"Nice to make your acquaintance, Miss..."

"Isles," she replies, shaking his proffered hand firmly. "Harley Isles."

He smiles, and it's warm and fatherly, with none of the manic energy Mom brings to the room. "A good, solid name. Don't let my wife scare you off, Harley. Devon is our only child, which means we can come on strong at times."

The tension fades from around Harley's eyes. "I don't scare easy. I've been in the ring more than seventy times, and it takes a lot to get to me."

"Oh?" He peers at her more closely. "I see the

170

scars here"—he gestures to her forehead—"and here"—to her brows. "Is that from MMA?"

She shakes her head. "Muay thai. I've just returned from training in Thailand for years."

Pops whistles. "That's a lot of commitment."

She nods. "Once I commit to something, I give it my all."

Her gaze creeps toward me, but when she sees me looking, it skates away. My chest flutters. I want that. I want her to give me her all. Hopefully tonight is another step in the right direction.

"Goodness." Mom's hand rests over her heart. "How unique you are. I can see why Devon likes you." She turns to Pops. "Can you escort our guest to the table? I'll dish up the food and be there soon."

I thread my fingers through Harley's and squeeze her hand. "Thank you," I murmur, low enough not to be overhead.

"For what?"

"Staying calm."

A smirk twists her lips, too evil for my liking. "Thank me after I've finished digging up all the embarrassing childhood stories you never wanted anyone to hear."

# Chapter Twenty

*HARLEY*

We sit at a square dining table, one person per side, and Mrs. Green sets a plate in front of each of us. A familiar roast. I glance at Devon, and one side of his mouth hitches up.

"It smells great," I say to fill the silence. "By the way, you did a great job of teaching Devon to cook. He made your famous roast for me a while back."

"He did?" She sounds delighted. "I'm so glad he remembers how. I had my doubts."

"So, dear." Mr. Green pours us each a glass of lemon water. "Do you plan on being a professional fighter forever, or do you intend to settle down and have children?"

I break into a coughing fit, startled by the question. Who the hell even asks that kind of thing five minutes after meeting someone? Once I've caught my breath, I take a few seconds to think before answering.

"Not forever. My body will wear out eventually. But I want to be involved in the sport. Perhaps in a coaching or umpiring role." I don't respond to the question about kids, because honestly, they don't figure into my plan right now. Maybe they will eventually—who knows, I might discover a maternal streak—but I'm not planning for them, and I'm not comfortable discussing that kind of major life decision with people I hardly know.

"Devon." His mother turns to him. "Will you say grace?"

I watch as the others bow their heads and press their hands together, and I mimic the action. Devon murmurs a few words, and then they collectively say "Amen." I wait until Mr. Green takes his first bite before digging in, unsure of the proper protocol.

The food is even better than Devon's, and I make sure Mrs. Green knows how much I enjoy it. After a while, I decide it's time to steer the conversation where I want it to go.

"Tell me about Devon when he was younger." I send him a sly look. "I want to know all the embarrassing stories."

He rolls his eyes but doesn't seem overly concerned by what they might say.

Mrs. Green wipes her mouth on a napkin. "Devon has always been accident prone."

"I'm not sure that's quite the right phrase for it," Mr. Green adds. "More like, fate had it out for him."

My eyes widen. This sounds good. "How so?"

"His life has been a series of near misses." Mrs. Green cuts her potatoes as she speaks. "That's why we never understood it when he took up martial arts. He was always the child who fell down, broke bones, and got back out there like it never happened." Her tone is laced with affection, and something squeezes in my chest. Even if she doesn't understand him, she loves him very much. "It got worse as he grew older. He fell from the roof when he was cleaning the gutters. Was in a car wreck a couple of years ago and walked away with only a few scratches. Then there was that time he walked in on a burglar…"

She trails off, and Mr. Green picks up the story. "The guy had a knife, but Devon thought it would be a great idea to tackle him anyway. He had to get twelve stitches in his arm afterward."

"But I caught the guy," Devon says, as though that's the most relevant part. "Subdued him until the police could arrive."

"It was foolish," his mother snaps, her voice cracking with emotion.

"We lived to tell the tale." Devon is being his usual flippant self, and it's going down like a lead balloon with his parents.

Desperate to find a lighter subject, I ask, "What about during high school? Did he go through an awkward phase?"

Mrs. Green's lips purse more tightly. "My son doesn't know the meaning of awkward. He was born with an internal compass that seems to steer him through every situation he comes across."

"I've noticed that," I murmur, more to myself than them. I smile at Devon. "So am I to believe you're incredibly lucky, or incredibly unlucky?"

"Lucky," he says at the same time that both of his parents reply, "Unlucky."

And now I have mixed feelings. I wish I hadn't opened this topic. It makes me wonder though… if he's as reckless as they say, is my heart one of the things he's going to be reckless with?

"Hopefully, you'll have a calming effect on him." This comes from Mr. Green. "Help him see that there's more to life than MMA."

I snort because I'm the last person they should be looking to for that. "Actually, I love training, and I can see why he's gone down the path he has."

Not for the first time, Mrs. Green's expression makes me wonder if I sprouted an alien head. "Why is that?"

"It's a lot of fun. It's satisfying, and frankly, the adrenaline rush can be addictive." I smile at Devon, and his answering smolder gives me butterflies. It's grateful and adoring, and just as compelling as adrenaline. "I think training is what saved me."

"Saved you?" she echoes uncertainly.

"Yeah." I seem to be making a habit of opening up lately and I'm not sure what to make of it. "I was the daughter of a broke single mom. She gave me everything she could, but my childhood was tough. When I started at the local gym, I found a reason to feel good about myself. Something to give me meaning. I don't know where I might have ended up otherwise."

For a long minute, no one speaks. I swallow, uncomfortable, hoping I didn't ruin dinner.

"Oh, darling." Mrs. Green's eyes light with sympathy, and I barely resist the urge to squirm. "We're so grateful that the Lord brought martial arts into your life to save you and bring you to us today."

I nod, appreciating the sentiment but not convinced it was God who steered me into a dingy gym frequented by men with more tattoos than teeth. It's a pretty thought, though.

---

*HARLEY*

Much later, when Devon and I are lying in bed after I've ridden him to orgasm, I rest my cheek over

175

his heart and ask the questions that have been on my mind all evening.

"How did you get into MMA? And when did you meet Seth?"

He presses his lips to the top of my head and everything inside me liquefies. I'm just a puddle of melty goo in human form.

"One of my friends took me along to his gym when we were in high school. It felt like coming home. Like I belonged somewhere for once. I did it in secret for a while because Mom and Pops didn't approve. Then, one day, the coach suggested I try my luck in the ring. I did. Had to forge one of my parents' signatures because I was still a minor." He strokes his fingers along the side of my face. "Do you think poorly of me for that?"

"No." I kiss his pec. "We do what we have to. No judgment here." But I do wonder how a guy like him could ever feel out of place anywhere. He's a natural people-person.

"Thanks." A breath rattles out of him, as if he's relieved. "I met Seth a few years later, when Jase and I faced off. He kicked my ass, but he'd been on the scene for longer and apparently Seth saw something in me he liked because he offered me a spot at Crown MMA. That was that. Until recently, I couldn't imagine being anywhere else."

I wince. "I'm sorry you had to leave, even if it's temporary."

He sighs. "When are you going to figure out that you mean more to me than a place?"

"I think you need to kiss me a few more times first."

He chuckles, and brushes his lips over mine. "Better?"

"Almost," I tease. "So tell me, what was it like starting at Crown MMA as a relative newbie?"

"Honestly, I loved it. I fit with the people there better than I ever have with Mom and Dad, much as I love them."

I tilt my head up to meet his gaze. "They do seem to have different priorities than you."

"You have no idea."

"What you said before…" I'm not sure how to broach this. "About belonging somewhere for once. What did you mean by that?"

He rolls one shoulder, his muscles stiffening almost imperceptibly. "I always got along well enough with my friends and the kids at school, but I felt like I was playing a role. At the gym, I was free to be the real me. Do I sound crazy?"

"Not at all." I snuggle closer into him. "I know exactly what you mean."

His body relaxes, and he exhales softly. "That's why you're perfect for me."

"I hope so," I whisper, so quietly I'm not sure he hears it. "So," I continue, more loudly, "you haven't introduced any other women to your parents. Was there anyone serious they didn't know about?"

He toys with the tips of my hair. "Not before you."

*Eep.* There he goes again. Muddling up my feelings. But this time, I like it.

"What about you?" he asks. "Other than He Who Shall Not Be Named, has there been anyone serious in your life?"

"Plenty." When he glares down at me, I add, "You've seen how serious Seth is."

He groans. "I meant romantically."

My mouth tips up. "Then you should have been specific."

Eye roll.

"But no, there hasn't been. The high school guys were frightened of me because I hung around with grown men who could kick their asses. Then, in Thailand, I wasn't exactly on the prowl. Don't get me wrong, I wasn't a virgin before Thaklaew, but I'd never been on more than a couple of dates with the same guy either."

"Good." I can feel his breath on my hairline when he speaks. "Does that mean I'm special?"

I smooth a hand over his chest. "Digging for compliments?"

"Shamelessly."

"Yes." Angling my face up, I kiss the line of his jaw. "I can honestly say I've never met anyone like you."

I'm beginning to think I never will again, that regardless of how different we might seem on the outside, he's it for me.

And that both thrills and terrifies me.

# Chapter Twenty-One

*HARLEY*

For the next two weeks—except for when we part ways during the day, each going to our separate gym—Devon and I are practically glued at the hip. We run together, lift weights together, talk tactics together, and then screw against every available surface of his apartment. It's insane. I should be tired of him, but I don't ever remember enjoying myself so much, and he doesn't seem to be losing interest in me either. Not to mention that I've had more orgasms since we started sleeping together than I've had in my life before him. My sexcapades have never been particularly successful and he puts every other man I've been with to shame.

Seth hasn't come around yet, but I've been casually mentioning Devon on the occasions when I visit his condo to restock my clothing or do the laundry. Honestly, I may as well move into Devon's place at the rate we're going. I also drop his name into conversation at the gym. Mention what his training plans are. What strategy we're working on for his fight. So far, I haven't made much headway, but we have progressed from

Seth raising an eyebrow each time I bring it up to grunting in acknowledgement and looking mildly interested, which means he's desperately curious on the inside.

It's a Friday evening, and Devon and I are cuddled on his sofa, alternating between watching Karson Hayes's past fights and watching those of my potential opponents. We're analyzing them. Sharing opinions, advice, and commentary. On the screen, Tammy Haddon—one of the women in my tournament— slams an opponent to the ground and straddles her.

"She's too aggressive," Devon comments. "Not great on defense."

Rich coming from him. I watch as Tammy pulverizes the girl beneath her. "Can't argue with the results."

He shakes his head. "You can take her. She's not one of the bigger threats."

We've been coming up with a tactic for each girl I might face, and prioritizing them from smallest to biggest threat. This is probably stuff I should be doing with Seth, and I'm sure he'll approach me about it at some stage, but there's something comforting about talking it through with Devon first. He has such unwavering faith in me and seems invested in helping me come out on top.

The fight ends, and we switch to another one with Karson Hayes. I have to say, I like seeing the blond egomaniac getting punched in the face by some guy named Taz, who's easily bigger than him. He seemed like a douchebag when he cornered me at Steel Angels, and having heard what happened between him and Lena only confirms that impression. I'm all about helping Devon kick his ass.

"He doesn't like it when people get in the pocket," I remark.

Devon nods. "Good spotting. I need to work on my uppercuts and knees."

I love that he listens to my advice. A lot of men seem to think they can't benefit by taking advice from a woman—even if that woman has had more than twice as much experience as them—but he just listens. No crying about his ego. To be honest, I think it's rock solid, which means there's no need for him to be bothered by my suggestions.

We watch Karson come out with the win—much to my disappointment—then swap to another girl from my list. The fight we choose has a lot of jiu-jitsu style grappling. The knot of nerves in my gut cinches tighter.

"I'm not sure I'm on her level when it comes to this stuff," I admit. Showing weakness isn't high up on my list of favorite pastimes, but I'm trying to get better at being vulnerable with him.

"You'll get there," he assures me, then adds, "Even if you don't, I'll still love you if you have cauliflower ears and a smooshed nose."

My mouth falls open and my chest tightens. "You'll what?"

I can tell he doesn't even realize what he's admitted. Slowly, he turns to face me, ignoring the action on the screen.

"What did you just say?" I persist, unable to think of anything except his absentminded comment.

He studies me for a long moment, dozens of micro-expressions flickering across his face before his mouth slowly curves up at the edges. "I'll still love you no matter how much grappling messes you up."

"You…" I can hardly manage to say the word. "Love me?"

"I do." He seems almost as surprised by this declaration as I am, but then he shrugs and returns to being the Devon I'm used to. "I've never been one to hide my feelings, so why start now?"

I stare at him, my brain short-circuiting. He's just dumped the "L" word on us. How am I supposed to process that?

Now he's looking at me expectantly, and all I can do is panic. Do I love him? Based on my talk with Ashlin, I think it's possible I do, but I'm not sure what love looks like. Familial love, sure. But not romantic love.

---

*DEVON*

Yup. It's official. I've shocked Harley into silence.

I'm not surprised. I wasn't expecting to confess my feelings for her. I didn't consciously know they went that deep. It just slipped out, but as soon as I thought about it, I realized it was true, and even if I could take it back, I wouldn't. Loving her feels right, and it's not just surface-level infatuation like when we first met. I love her for who she is, where she's been, and where she wants to go. I love her for her prickly attitude and ability to kick a grown man's ass.

I'm not afraid to let her know it, either. If she doesn't feel the same way yet, that's fine, but she and I have come a long way and I trust she'll get there. Gazing into her eyes, admiring every single gold fleck amongst the green and brown, I know with utter certainty that I'd announce my feelings to the whole damn world if I could.

"That's…" Her voice shakes, and she seems awed. "That's huge. Are you sure?"

Resisting the urge to roll my eyes because only she would ask that, I nod. "Harley Isles, I'm madly fucking in love with you."

She kisses me.

Pours her whole heart and soul into it.

This is a kiss to end all kisses.

It doesn't escape my notice that she never returns the sentiment, but she climbs onto my lap, already breathing heavily, desperate for me. If this is the only way she can express herself, I'm not going to turn her away. I'm going to accept everything she's trying to show me through her actions.

"Hold on a sec." Reaching around her, I flick off the screen so there's no chance of me catching sight of Karson Hayes when I'm mid-orgasm. Then I return to her, kissing the length of her throat, grazing my teeth over the juncture of her neck and shoulder. She shudders. Her knees are on either side of my thighs, her pussy nestled over my cock, a few layers of fabric separating them. She's only wearing her panties, having kicked off her jeans when we started snuggling. I cup my palm over her, feeling how wet she is through the thin covering. When I stroke her, she moans brokenly.

"All of this is for me?" I ask.

"Yes," she whispers, rocking her hips and riding my hand. My cock strains against my zipper, wanting to break free. Wanting inside her.

"Get them off," I order.

She doesn't move, still rocking, chasing bliss. It seems like I'll have to take care of things myself.

"Don't say I didn't warn you." I grab the waistband of her panties in both hands and rend the fabric. She gasps, and at first I think she's outraged, but then she throws her head back and laughs. The sound is husky and makes me even harder. Rolling my hips, I scrape the rough denim of my jeans over her bare pussy and her laughter ends abruptly. She catches her lower lip between her teeth and whimpers, then I repeat the motion, and her eyes darken into molten desire. I glance at my crotch. Her arousal has dampened it, and seeing the evidence that she's so turned on she's dripping all over me turns me into a starving wolf.

"Holy shit, honey," I groan, and in a smooth motion, I flip her onto her back, yank her tank top off, and unfasten her bra so I can see all of her. She lies back, arms up above her head, gripping onto the back of the sofa. Settling between her legs, my gaze drops to the decadent treat I'm dying to taste. "Look at you." My voice is a rasp. "Fucking delicious."

Unable to resist for any longer, I lower my mouth over her pussy and lick her center. She cries out.

"Mm," I hum in the back of my throat. Just as amazing as I remember. "Need more."

I go all in, licking and sucking and teasing, driving her higher and higher. But then she plants a foot on my chest and pushes me away before she can come, her eyes wild, chest heaving.

"Fuck me," she orders, her lower lip pouty from where her teeth have been digging into it as she holds in the noises that want to spill out.

"Yes, ma'am."

Her eyes narrow, but then I strip off my jeans and stark need replaces the annoyance. In a graceful movement, she rolls over the arm of the sofa and parts her thighs, her forearms on the cushions, her slit exposed for me to take her from behind.

"You want it like that?" I ask.

She nods and arches her back, her ass tempting me. I'm a quick study so I position myself behind her, on my knees, and notch my cock at her entrance.

"Wait," she groans just as I'm about to enter her. "Condom."

*Fuck.* I can't believe I nearly forgot. Shifting away, I dig in my wallet and slip the protection on, then resume my position. Swaying forward, I press into her an inch at a time. Her breath hitches with each thrust until I'm lodged firmly inside, and she murmurs my name, followed by, "Oh God."

I bottom out in her. "You feel like the best thing ever."

"You're better," she gasps, pushing back to meet me halfway.

We keep up the back-and-forward for all of two minutes before I can't take any more. I grab her hips and fuck her like an animal. Grunting. Rutting. Heat lashes down my spine as I get closer and closer. She urges me on with sexy little noises, then her pussy contracts around me and she cries out. It feels too good and I hurtle into oblivion. This time, my heart follows my body over the edge and I give her everything I have. No holding back. No regrets.

Hopefully she'll be waiting for me at the bottom.

# Chapter Twenty-Two

*Devon*

When I arrive home after a long training session, I find Harley lying on the sofa, staring at the ceiling. She's lost in thought and doesn't glance up as I approach. I come to a stop above her.

"Harls, you okay?"

She flinches, then smiles sheepishly. "Sorry, you surprised me. I didn't hear you come in."

"I wasn't exactly quiet." I never am. "Quiet" isn't a strength of mine. "What's going on in that head of yours?"

"I've been thinking."

"About what?" I perch on the edge of the sofa, looking down at her.

"About my mom." She purses her lips. "I haven't seen her for ages, and meeting your parents got me thinking about her. She visited in Thailand a while ago, but I haven't gone home since getting back into the country, and I probably should."

"Huh." She rarely mentions her mom, and neither

does Seth. I don't even know the woman's name. "Is she local?"

"No." Something flashes in her eyes that looks a lot like vulnerability. "She's in a little town called Cedar Bend in Oregon."

"Cedar Bend," I muse. "It sounds like something from a Hallmark film."

She snorts. "Hardly. It's one of those places with a very clear line between the haves and the have-nots, and when I was young, we fell firmly on the wrong side of that line. An irredeemable flaw as far as many of the locals are concerned."

"Surely your mom isn't on the wrong side of that line anymore," I say, fishing for more information. I want to know where she came from and what made her who she is. "What with Seth being a big name and having his own gym."

"Nah, Seth may have bought her a nice house in a good part of town, but that doesn't make the locals treat her any better. Her son made his money with his fists." Her face twists with scorn. "Not a respectable career, in their holier-than-thou opinions."

"Fuck them. Anyone who judges people based on money and circumstances isn't worth her time."

Her smile is full of gratitude and it hits me with the power of a foot to the gut. "You're right. Fuck 'em. Who cares what they think anyway?"

"Exactly." I nod, encouraging her. "But you should definitely visit, and you should bring me with you."

She smiles, almost shyly. "I was hoping you'd say that."

"I want to see where the woman I love grew up." I don't hold back on reminding her of how I feel. Even if she doesn't love me yet, she cares deeply. "I want to see the house where you grew up, visit your school, have tea with your mom, or whatever the fuck people do in Cedar Bend, Oregon. Because I want to know you."

She shifts restlessly. "You do. More than most people." She sits up, swings her legs around until her thighs align with mine, and grabs her phone from her pocket. "I was actually thinking of visiting next weekend. Just a flying trip. What do you say?"

"Hell, yeah." I pump my fist. "Will Seth want to come?" I haven't seen my old coach since he found out about me and Harley, although he's sent me a couple of texts with suggestions about combinations to use against Karson Hayes, which I'm taking as a positive sign.

"Uh, no." She sighs. "He never visits Mom. He always gets her to travel down here. He hates Cedar Bend. I always feel bad for Mom though. It must be hard for her."

I squeeze her thigh. "He'll go there eventually. Maybe he just doesn't like losing the time it takes to travel. He's a busy guy."

"No." She shakes her head, her voice strained. "Trust me, it's not that. There are some deep issues I don't want to get into."

"Okay." I'm intrigued, but I won't pry. "Either way, I'm glad I get to come."

Her lips curve up. "Me, too."

Is it crazy how excited I am?

Yeah, probably. I should be crapping myself because I'm about to meet my future mother-in-law, but I couldn't be happier. Bring on next weekend. I'm going to show Ms. Isles how much I deserve her daughter.

*HARLEY*

After training wraps up the following Saturday, Devon and I pack our gear and head to the airport. It's a short flight to Portland, and from there, we hire a car and drive to Cedar Bend. During the commute, I have plenty of time to wonder how this is going to go. Just as I was the first woman Devon had brought home, he's the first boyfriend I've introduced to my mother.

I sneak a glance at him. One of his arms is draped over the steering wheel, and the other stretches across the space between us, his palm facing up. I rest mine atop it and he closes his fingers. Warmth rushes through me. Even that slight gesture of affection has a cozy, snuggly sensation lighting me up inside.

"How are you doing?" he asks. "You've been quiet."

"I'm good. Just thinking."

"Ugh, thinking." He chuckles. "A surefire way to start doubting yourself. Dare I ask what you're thinking about?"

I study the angle of his jaw. So familiar. So handsome. I ache to kiss along the line of it. "You." I can tell I've surprised him when he doesn't reply immediately.

"Are they good thoughts or bad thoughts?"

"Good." Raising his hand, I kiss the back of his knuckles. "Definitely good."

"That's a relief." He swallows, and I have the insane urge to run my hand down his abs and dip it beneath his waistband, but I don't want to distract him while he's driving. "I don't suppose you'd care to share?"

I wink when he turns to me briefly. "Nope."

"Be like that then." He pretends to pout, and it's so

ridiculous I snort-laugh. "So, tell me. What was your favorite thing about growing up in Cedar Bend?"

"The gym." I don't even have to think about it. "Cedar Bend Martial Arts."

"It has a certain ring to it." His thumb draws a languid circle on the back of my hand. "What did you love about it so much?"

I shrug because it's easier to do that than to try to tamp down all of the uncomfortable memories flying back at me. "It was like family, I guess. When I first turned up, not long after Seth left town, they didn't think I belonged there, but I stuck it out, and by the time I left, those rough old guys were like my surrogate dads."

"That's cool." He stares out the windshield at the road as the landscape whirs by. "Why'd you start going after Seth left? Seems like something you would have done together."

I laugh. "You ask a lot of questions." He just looks at me, and I fidget. "Seth used to stand up for me, and scare away the bullies who thought it was fun to torment a scrawny poor girl. But he left town the moment he turned eighteen and I was on my own."

He hums in sympathy. "You must have been young."

"Six or seven. Apparently, I found my way to his old gym and insisted they teach me." My lips quirk at the thought. I don't really remember it, but I made quite an impression. "One of them, Don, took me home, but I kept coming back, and eventually Mom got them to agree to let me stay for the classes." By the time I reached high school, most of my peers were scared of me. It made things lonely, but I don't want Devon's pity so I don't mention that.

"So, you were always a stubborn little thing."

"Yup. Guilty."

He chuckles, and the rich sound makes me want to curl up in his lap. God, it's inconvenient being this attracted to someone. "Seriously, I think you're amazing. I'm sorry you had it rough, but you grew into a kickass woman, and I love you for it. Is it weird that I kinda want to visit your gym and shake those men's hands?"

"Maybe," I answer. "But not in a bad way. Now, enough questions about me. I want to hear what you were like growing up."

"A nightmare." His reply is swift and certain. "It's a miracle my parents didn't leave me on the side of the road somewhere. I was one of those full-steam-ahead kids who destroy everything in their paths."

"That sounds about right." I can picture him. Small, with brown eyes and a mischievous smile, knocking things down while looking so damned cute his parents couldn't do a thing about it. "You're a very open person. Why is that?" It's only because I'm watching him so closely that I see a muscle tick in his jaw. "Dev, you okay?"

He exhales slowly, as though he's counting in his head, then he says, "I was adopted. It's not a big thing, but I didn't find out until I was a teenager, and it hit me kind of hard, so I prefer not to put anyone in a situation where they don't know the full truth."

"Oh." My brow scrunches. "So your mom and dad aren't actually—"

"My biological parents," he finishes. "But I don't care about that. We love each other, even if we don't always understand each other. It was actually a relief when I found out, because I'd always wondered why I was so different from them, and I finally had a reason."

I moisten my lips before speaking, afraid I'm going

to say the wrong thing. His entire body is tense, and I can tell this is a difficult subject for him. "Then why was it so hard?"

"Because…" His eyes slide over to mine for the barest moment., "I wasted all that time and energy worrying about whether something was wrong with me for being so different from them when I didn't need to. If they'd just told me sooner, it would have saved me a lot of angst."

Shame burns in my chest because a lot of things make sense with this new information. Like why being untruthful with Seth was so difficult for him. I forced him into a situation that must have eaten him up with guilt. It fundamentally went against what he believes in.

"I'm sorry," I whisper, hoping he'll understand.

His tension doesn't ease, but his expression relaxes into an almost-smile. "You're worth it, and the deception didn't last for long."

I nod, wishing I could take it all back anyway. One thing is for sure: there's a whole lot more to Devon Green than I initially gave him credit for.

When we arrive in Cedar Bend, it's dark, so we decide to save the tour until tomorrow. I issue directions to Mom's place, which is a large house made of white stone down by the river that divides the town in two. Seth had it built for her with his winnings back when he was a regular on the professional circuit. Devon pulls up the long drive and parks in a graveled area beside the house.

He whistles. "Nice place. How much of your childhood did you spend here?"

I study it for differences, but it looks much the same as it used to. "Most of my teenage years."

"I bet all of your friends wanted to come over."

"I didn't really have any," I admit, trying to be honest with him after his confession earlier.

Pushing the car door open, I hop out before he can reply. I don't need pity. He comes around the front of the car and grabs my hand just as the outside light flickers on. The front door flies open and Mom races out, the wind shifting her blonde hair in a fluffy cloud around her face. Where Seth and I are both tall, she's short, barely coming up to my nose as she wraps her arms around me. She squeezes me tight, rocking from side to side, then releases me and steps back, grinning broadly. While I didn't get my height from her, I did get her coloring. The eyes beaming up at me, while narrower than mine, are the exact same shade.

"Honey!" she exclaims, scanning my face as if to catalog all the changes since I saw her last. "I'm so glad you're here." She hauls me into another hug. "Ugh, I can't believe it's been so long." I return the embrace, smelling the welcome lavender scent of her. When she lets me go, she turns to Devon. "You must be Devon." She extends a hand toward him. He takes it and pulls her into a hug, startling a laugh from her.

"It's an honor to meet you, Ms. Isles." He steps back and gives her a shy smile that has my heart flipping over in my chest. "Wow, you look just like Harley."

Mom giggles, then claps a hand to her mouth. "I can see why my daughter likes you." She gestures toward the entrance. "Come in. I'll make us a hot drink. Do you prefer coffee, tea, or hot chocolate?"

"Whatever is easiest." He opens the trunk and grabs our bags, slinging one over each shoulder.

"How about you, honey?" she asks.

"Tea, please."

She leads us inside, through a foyer with a tiled

floor, and down a long hall to one of the spare bedrooms. "Put your things in here and get settled. I'll make those drinks."

She leaves, and Devon drops the bags and rounds on me, caging me against the wall with his muscular arms. His forehead rests against mine, and our breath intermingles.

"I need to kiss you," he murmurs.

I press my lips to his and arch into his body. His arms slide down the wall and loop around my lower back, drawing me close to him. His tongue delves into my mouth, tasting me, and my breath hitches when the ridge of his erection presses against my core. Sighing, I place a hand on his chest and ease him back.

"Whoa, cowboy. Better get things under control before we go back out."

He nods, but holds me tight to his chest. "I love you, Harley. Thank you for this."

"Thank you for coming." For the first time since he originally said he loved me, I don't feel like I have to reply in kind—but I want to. I force myself to keep the words inside until I have a chance to examine them and figure out what's going on in my head. "Come on."

Threading my fingers through his, I walk with him to the living room, where I sit on one of the massive couches and tuck my feet up beneath me. Devon takes an armchair, and I have to admit, I'm disappointed to lose his touch. It's for the best though. I don't want to make Mom uncomfortable. A few moments later, she emerges from the kitchen, carrying a tray with a teapot and three cups on it. She sets the tray on the coffee table and pours tea into each cup.

"It's chamomile," she says. "Didn't want to caffeinate you right before bed."

"Thanks, Ms. Isles." Devon takes one of the teacups, which looks ridiculous in his large hand.

"Please, call me Mae." She passes me one of the teacups and claims the last one for herself. "How long have you two been an item?"

"Not long." I share a glance with Devon. "We're still very new. Devon was actually a fighter at Crown MMA, but Seth said he had to leave when we told him about our relationship. He didn't want us bringing any drama into the gym."

Mom rolls her eyes. "Of course he did. That son of mine doesn't know the meaning of compromise." She smiles. "Don't worry, he'll get used to the idea eventually."

She sits cross-legged on the couch beside me. "So, tell me about when you first met. Is there a cute story?"

I indicate for Devon to tell her, and before I know it, two hours have passed while we sit and talk and laugh. He seems to have charmed his way into Mom's good graces—she's been catching my eye every now and then to share a woman-to-woman communication that says things like "good job!", "he's great!", and "hold onto him." But the killer moment comes when it's time to clean up and the three of us take our dishes to the kitchen. Mom tries to turn the faucet on and curses when it doesn't do anything.

"Let me take a look," Devon offers. While Mom and I watch, he checks out the plumbing, then requests a wrench, and within a few short minutes, the faucet works like it should.

As he tests it out, Mom leans closer and whispers to me, "He's lovely. Don't let him go."

My heart is full to bursting, and I can't look away from him. The sleeves of the button-down shirt he insisted on wearing to make a good impression are rolled up, exposing strong forearms dusted with hair, and a tiny bit of tongue pokes out the corner of his mouth as he concentrates. He's so gorgeous it almost hurts to look at him, but that isn't what's choking me up. All of the feelings I've been denying have slammed into me with the force of a brick wall, knocking me off balance and stealing the air from my lungs.

*I love him.*

I do.

It's like there's been this sensation deep inside me, fighting to get to the surface and it's finally broken through.

Devon is a guy who fixes things without being asked. Who's honest and open about everything—far more than I've ever been. Who's playful and trustworthy. He isn't going to hurt me because he's someone worth loving.

# Chapter Twenty-Three

*Devon*

Harley stretches out next to me in the double bed her mother assigned us for the night. Her hand wanders up my torso, her gentle touch awakening parts of me I've tried to put to sleep.

"Are you sure you don't want to?" she asks. "She probably assumes we are, anyway."

"I'm sure." Taking her hand, I curl mine around it to stop its journey over my sensitive skin. "I can't face Mae tomorrow morning if I spend the night banging her daughter. You'll have to rein in your libido for one night. I know it'll be a struggle," I tease, "when you've got all this sexy goodness in bed with you, but you'll manage."

She nips my shoulder. "Oh, I'll manage. You're the one who can't go a night without sex."

I stifle a laugh because we both know we're equally insatiable. She loves the physical side of our relationship as much as I do. Unfortunately, I don't have much experience with meeting the parents of women I'm dating—because I don't usually see them more than a few times—and it just seems like good etiquette to keep my dick out of Harley while under Mae Isles's roof. Not to mention that I like Mae, and I want her to like me too.

Smoothing a hand over Harley's hair, I kiss the top of her head, and then twirl a loose strand around my finger. "What were your dreams?" I ask softly. "When you were a kid, where did you want your life to go?"

"That's a deep question for when I'm half asleep." She's quiet for several seconds, and I wonder if that's all she's going to say on the matter, but then she continues. "Promise you won't think this is corny?"

"Promise." I have no idea what she's about to say, but I'm eager to learn more about the girl she was when she lived in this big, welcoming house.

She sighs, and her breath tickles my chest. "I wanted to find a place to belong. That was it. I didn't have any big ambitions, I just wanted to fit in somewhere and be liked and accepted for who I was."

My heart expands, threatening to burst out of my ribcage because her dream so closely mirrors my own. I never realized quite how much I felt like I didn't fit until I found somewhere I did.

"Oh, baby." I drop another kiss on her forehead. "And did you?"

"I thought I did." Her voice is so quiet I can hardly hear her. "But Thaklaew ruined that."

If I ever meet this Thaklaew guy, I'm going to punch him in the face. It's better than he deserves. "What about at Crown MMA?"

Her chin angles up, and in the dark, I can barely see the shining of her eyes. "Maybe one day."

"It used to be my place to belong," I confess. "I hope it will be again, but like I've said, it's not the end of the world if it isn't. I didn't have such a hard time growing up as you, but I felt out of place in my own family, even though I never doubted they loved me. Seth has built a tightknit community, and I felt like part of it. Yeah, the guys think I'm a little crazy, but they see me, flaws and all, and they call me their brother anyway."

At least, they used to—and hopefully still do.

I've seen Jase and Gabe a few times recently, and our friendship doesn't seem damaged by my change of circumstances. Honestly, I do love those guys, and I'm grateful every day that I found my way to them.

"That's really beautiful," she says, and snuggles closer. "I'm sure you'll have it again once Seth's finished being an ass. What was your dream when you were growing up?"

I grin. "To be a stunt double in action movies."

She laughs, as I knew she would, and my soul lightens. "Go figure. I can totally see that."

I slide my arm down to her waist. It's impossible to move her any closer, but if I could, I would. "Strange how we had such different dreams but ended up in the same place. Must be fate."

She snorts, and even though I can't see in the dark, I imagine she rolls her eyes. She doesn't say anything though, and we lie together as the minutes slip away. I feel restful and at peace, but not at all sleepy, and based on the way her breathing doesn't even out into a slow rhythm, I'd wager she's in the same situation.

"I love you."

Her words are soft but echo like a gunshot in the silence. My pulse accelerates, spiking me into full wakefulness. I open my mouth then close it, uncertain how to respond, and praying that I heard her right.

"I love you, Devon," she repeats, more clearly.

Twisting around, I kiss her, nearly missing her lips.

Oh, my God, I can't believe she said it. She wouldn't, unless she were one hundred percent certain, which means that she truly loves me. Beyond a doubt.

"I love you, too," I reply as I separate my lips from hers. "So damn much." My arms tighten around her. "Thank you. You've given me something wonderful, and I swear I'll take care of it."

"I know you will." She kisses my jaw, and I swallow, her proximity and confession wreaking havoc on my self-control. I want to kiss her senseless and then fuck her until she screams how much she loves me while she comes. But I hold back.

"When did you know?" I wonder aloud.

"Honestly?" Her hand settles over my heart, which is beating steadily for her. "When you fixed the faucet."

I burst out laughing, and she shoves a hand over my mouth to hush me. I kiss her palm, and she recoils.

"That is such a you thing to say." It's practical, and a little odd, which only makes me adore her more. How many people could say they fell in love watching someone manhandle their mother's wrench?

She pouts. "Don't make fun of me."

I stop dead. "I'm not. It's perfect." And then, because I can, I add, "I love you."

When she replies, "I love you, too," I could shout with joy.

I'm jubilant, and I want to demand she pack her things and officially move into my place as soon as we get back. But because I'm mostly sane—despite what some people think—I press my lips together and keep the demands to myself. I'll wait for a better time, when she won't feel like it's too much, too fast.

But hopefully, it'll be sooner than we both expect.

In the morning, after having breakfast with Mom and hugging her goodbye, I show Devon around Cedar Bend. First, we drive past the school. In my memories, the brick buildings ringing the sports field are larger and more intimidating. Prison-like. In reality, they're drab and worn but nothing scary. My imagination must have inflated them because of the dread I felt coming through the gates each day.

"So this is where the Isles siblings learned their ABCs," Devon remarks, craning his neck out the window as we slow to a crawl.

"Yep. The one part of Cedar Bend I'd happily never enter again."

He gets the hint, and puts his foot on the gas. "I want to see the gym you told me about. Does the man who coached you still work there?"

"He does." Don and I haven't really kept in touch, but he's sent me a few messages over the years to see how I'm doing, and I've worked with a couple of teenagers he shipped over to Thailand for a muay thai vacation. I give Devon directions to the gym, and he parks outside. My old home away from home is a squat concrete building with faded text across the wall above the doorway that reads, "Cedar Bend Martial Arts." Several cars are parked along the curb and music filters out through the open door. There's a class in session.

Devon turns to me, eyes sparkling with excitement. "Should we go in?"

"Let's do it." With determination, I climb out of the vehicle and stride toward the entrance. He jogs to catch up. Inside, I pause to take in the scene. Equipment lining the walls and filling the corners of the room, boxing bags hanging from the ceiling, and people spaced around the room in pairs. There's no ring. Nothing fancy. Just grassroots stuff. A sense of being home washes over me, and I inhale the familiar leather-and-sweat scent.

"Fake jab, low right," a man's voice booms, drawing my attention. He's older, his face worn and crinkled, his hair more salt than pepper and thinning on top, but I'd recognize Don anywhere. The pairs do as he says, one person throwing punches while the other holds pads. We pause in the doorway, watching. As if he senses us, Don glances over. Then, slowly, a smile transforms his face.

"Body kicks until the beeper," he calls, his legs eating up the distance between us.

"Hey, Don," I say, right before I'm yanked into a crushing hug. "Oomph."

He thrusts me back and holds me at arm's length, examining my features, apparently cataloging the scars I've accumulated over the years. "Harley fucking Isles." He shakes his head like he can't believe I'm here. "What's a girl like you doing in a place like this?"

I roll my eyes at the cheesy line. "Probably the same thing as an old coot like you, Donnie."

He winces. "Told you not to call me that."

Cocking my head, I grin. "Been a few years. Might've forgotten."

"Or maybe you like winding up an old man," he grouses, then kisses my cheek and releases me. "You look good, darlin'. Thailand agrees with you."

I wait for the heaviness to settle in my heart at the reminder of Thailand, but for the first time, it doesn't come. Perhaps I'm making progress.

"Haven't you heard? I'm in Las Vegas these days. Got my first fights in a few weeks."

His brow arches. "Do you now? Well then, I'll be watching."

Okay, that gives me a dose of the warm fuzzies. "I want to hear your thoughts afterward, just like the old days."

He chuckles. "It wasn't that long ago, kid. So tell me, whose gym are you fighting out of?"

"Seth's."

He does a double take. "MMA, huh? Never figured you for the type to like rollin' on the ground."

I shrug. "I'm learning."

Devon shifts beside me, and Don turns to him. It takes less than three seconds for recognition to set in.

"Well, damn," he exclaims. "If it isn't 'Dangerous' Devon Green." He holds out a hand, which Devon shakes firmly. "Don Chapman. Great to meet you. I've watched a few of your fights."

Devon's smile mirrors Don's. "Hopefully the good ones. It's an honor to meet the first man to teach my warrior princess how to throw a punch."

Don's gaze skitters back and forth between us. "You two are a thing?"

"Yeah," I admit.

"That's fucking fantastic." He pumps Devon's hand again, then wraps one arm around my shoulders. "I'm thrilled you visited while you were in town. It's good to see you, kid."

"You, too, Donnie." All of a sudden, I'm not ready to leave. I want to spend more time in this place that used to mean everything to me. "You know, Dev and I don't have to be anywhere for a few hours. Why don't we help out with your class?" Both men stare at me. "What do you say?" I ask Devon.

"I'm in." His answer comes easily, as I knew it would.

Don flushes pink with pleasure, but cautions us, "Once I introduce you to these troublemakers, you might not get away again for a while."

"Fine by me."

Shaking his head again, as if bemused by the entire situation, he pivots, and whistles to get everyone's attention. A dozen faces turn his way.

"We have some very special guests." He lays a hand on my shoulder, just like he used to, and for some ridiculous reason, it chokes me up. "This here is Harley Isles. She's just returned from living in Thailand, where she did professional muay thai." He angles his head toward me. "How many fights you had, Harley?"

"Seventy-six."

"*Seventy-six,*" he says, and a weighty silence follows. An atmosphere of anticipation fills the room. "It's not often you get the chance to learn from someone with that many bouts under their belt." A low murmur sounds. "And if you haven't already recognized him, this gentleman is Devon Green. He trains out of Crown MMA Gym in Las Vegas, under my former student Seth Isles." The murmur grows to a hum, the small group eying us with excitement. Then, with impeccable timing, Don delivers the knockout punch. "They're going to work with each of you this morning. Listen to them. Give them your respect. These guys know what they're talking about." Several of them pump their fists. One guy cheers aloud. Don lowers his voice as he addresses Devon and me. "How do you want to do this?"

"We could take each person through a couple of rounds on pads," Devon suggests.

"At the end, anyone who wants to try their hand at sparring us can have a go," I add.

"Perfect." Don winks. "Hope you're prepared for the fan-girling."

"I'm sure we'll survive."

An hour later, I'm less certain. I've fielded more questions about what it's like to train in Thailand than ever in my life, and Devon has accumulated a circle of adoring fans who are hanging on his every word. The two teenage girls seem particularly fond of him. If not for their youth and the sizzling looks he sends my way every time he has a chance, I might be concerned. They don't show their budding crushes by giggling and flirting. Rather they try to impress him with their stellar technique and ability to throw a punch that could make a grown man cry. I recognize the show of one-upmanship because I've been there. Strange as it sounds, there comes a time when being able to slip under a man's guard and deliver an uppercut to his jaw is equivalent to preening in a prom dress.

Don laps up the experience, and it makes my spirit light to see how much joy it brings him to have us here. Eventually, we have to leave. I extricate myself from the group and hug him tightly, breathing into his ear that it won't be so long before I come back again.

"See to it," he says, ruffling my hair. Then he shakes Devon's hand. "Don't let her walk all over you, and good luck to both of you with your fights."

"Thanks. Bye, Donnie."

"See you later, kid."

## Chapter Twenty-Four

*Devon*

I sink into a chair at Sugar, one of the cafés near Crown MMA Gym, opposite my future brother-in-law. Not that he or Harley realize it yet, but now that I have Harley's love, I'm hoping it's only a matter of time before I have her hand in marriage too. Oh, not immediately, but not far down the line.

"Hey, man. How are you doing?" I ask, reaching over to shake his hand. He grips mine firmly, then rests his elbow on the table and props his chin on his palm.

"Good. I was glad you called. We haven't talked for ages."

I smirk. "Well, you kicked me out of your gym, so…"

He winces. "I really am sorry about that. I was in a difficult position."

"Yeah, I know." I wave a hand. That isn't what I want to talk about today. It's a battle for another time.

"How was your trip to the fiery pit of hell?"

My lips twitch. "If you mean the sweet little town of Cedar Bend, it was nice." A server delivers me a savory roll and also places one in front of Seth, whose eyes narrow. I laugh. "Don't worry, it's free of sugar, refined starch, and flavor, just the way you like it."

He huffs as though annoyed, but we both know he loves my teasing.

"Your Mom is great."

"She is." His expression softens. "Everything went smoothly?"

"As silk." I dig into my food. "I also met your old trainer, Don. What a character."

He shakes his head. "Talk about taking me back. I haven't seen that guy in years. How's he doing?"

"Seems to be good."

Seth drinks from his glass of water and watches me thoughtfully. "Why did you want to meet?"

"Here's the thing." I wipe my fingers on a napkin and sit forward. I'm going to need steel balls for this. "I love Harley, and she loves me. I respect you, but I'd want to be with her regardless of your feelings on the matter. Still, I know she cares what you think and I don't want to damage her relationship with you, so I just want to ask directly: do you have a problem with her and I dating?"

He exhales slowly and rubs his bristly jaw. "No, Dev. I don't."

My heart starts beating again.

"Honestly," he continues, "when she first told me, I did wonder whether it was just a phase for you." He gives me a look. "You don't exactly have a rock-solid dating history. But it takes a lot of balls to ask what you just did, and I know you wouldn't have done that—or gone with her to visit Mom—if you weren't sure of your relationship. That's just not the kind of guy you are. You don't lead people on. So I don't have anything against you dating her." His lips twist so slightly at the corners that if he were anyone else, I might not notice, but Seth doesn't smile often, so it stands out. "I just don't like the situation it put me in, especially after I asked you both not to go there."

I shrug. "I'm sorry about that, but the heart wants what he wants."

He sighs. "That it does."

Something dark and sorrowful flashes across his face, but he hides it quickly. I wonder what it was about, and whether it has anything to do with his ex, Ashlin. I'm yet to meet her, but I'm curious to know more about the woman he married, and who befriended my Harley.

"You don't mind that she's cornering me?"

He quirks a brow. "She has the experience, and if she can stay objective when you're in the cage, then I don't see a problem." His gaze hardens. "Provided it doesn't interfere with her fights. She's my priority for the night."

I nod. "Got it. We'll make sure it doesn't."

"That's fine then." He takes another bite of his roll and chases it down with water. "Tell me how your training is going."

Hell, yeah. I grin. If he's asking, it means he cares. Maybe Seth and I are going to be all right after all.

---

*HARLEY*

One night. Five hours. Three fights.

At least, that's presuming I'm not eliminated.

I sip from my water bottle to wet my throat. The Nightshade event has rolled around faster than I ever imagined, and it's nearly time for my first bout. Seth, Jase, Gabe, and I arrive an hour early. I warm up, stretch, then spar with Jase while Gabe yells instructions. After that, I mop my face and lie still while a physiotherapist rubs me down with Thai oil. The spicy scent of it invades my nostrils and for a moment, it sends me right back to Thailand.

Closing my eyes, I visualize the fight ahead while the physio works my muscles over. My first opponent is Tammy Haddon, a bleached blonde with a nasty smirk and a lot of physical strength. Good on attack, weak on defense. I allow the upcoming match to play like a movie in my mind.

When the physio finishes with me, Seth wraps my hands.

"You've got this," he murmurs, one hundred percent of his attention focused on me. All of the awkwardness of the past two weeks has been put on hold for the sake of getting the win. "You've worked hard, and you have more fights under your belt than any of the others. Your grappling has been spot-on this week, and you know what you need to do." He meets my eyes briefly, his burning with intensity. "Tell me what the plan is for Tammy."

"Go forward," I answer automatically. "Put her on defense. Get her off balance."

"Good girl." He finishes one hand and moves to the other. I test the wrapping on the one that's complete. It's quite a change for me. I'm used to wearing lightweight boxing gloves, but these cage fighting knuckle-covers are completely different. There's much more freedom to move my fingers and also more ability to inflict serious damage.

My phone buzzes on the stool beside me. I check it. The message is from Devon, wishing me luck. There's a photo of his face to go with it, and I smile. Devon is somewhere in the building, although I haven't seen him yet. Ashlin volunteered to stay with him and help him get ready. Although she's never done MMA, she's well-schooled in the basics from years of being Seth's number one supporter.

Meanwhile, I'm facing pre-fight jitters. At least they're good for one thing. They prevent me from worrying about anything else.

Once I'm ready for action, a medic comes by to check me out. Declaring me good to go, she nods to a guy hovering in the doorway, who announces that it's time to make the walk to the stadium. The Nightshade event is in one of Vegas's smaller venues, with seating for a few thousand people. I put my mouthguard in and square my shoulders.

As we draw near the entrance into the arena, the song changes to metal music with a female singer. I gave Seth carte blanche to choose whichever walk-out song he wanted for me. I don't care what music is playing in the background. It's a hyped-up Western construct anyway. I enter the stadium, unsurprised when there aren't any cheers to greet me. I'm an unknown entity to these people, but by the end of the night, they'll be screaming my name.

A path has been cleared from the doorway into the center of the floor, where a raised cage is situated. I stride toward it, pausing at the base while my gloves and mouthguard are checked, then I climb the stairs and head for the far side. A couple of minutes later, Tammy joins me. She's older—perhaps in her thirties —with a nose that's been broken previously and a face that's seen its share of violence. When the fight begins, and my body settles into a familiar rhythm, her age and past don't matter. I dominate. The only moment when she's in control is the few seconds that she gets me into a hold I haven't practiced much, but even then, she's no match for me. Before the second round is over, she's tapped out. The umpire raises my hand in the air and declares me winner.

Out the back, Seth announces that my next fight will be against Savage Rose, the tattooed and shaven-headed woman I watched at the Steel Angels event. He ices my legs and the back of my neck. When I've cooled down, I tell him I need to check on Devon and duck out.

I find my man behind a door with his name taped to it. He's lying on the floor, face down, while Ashlin straddles him and rubs liniment and oil into his back. I take a moment to admire his gleaming brown muscles. My mouth waters. Damn, he's sexy, and it seems like forever since I felt him inside me because we've both been too preoccupied with the upcoming fights to light any fires between the sheets. Maybe tonight that will change. A delicate bud of hope blooms in my chest, and I nurture it until the door clicks shut behind me, alerting them both to my presence.

"Thanks, Ash," I say.

She shimmies down and starts on his thighs and calves. "No problem. I'm almost done. Congrats on your win."

"One down, two to go."

"You killed it out there," Devon calls, his voice muffled by the towel he's lying on. "Like a fucking battle queen. Great work getting out of that hold she had you stuck in."

"You noticed?" I'd thought I'd masked my trouble pretty well.

"I notice everything about you."

I want to kiss him, and my expression must say so because Ashlin huffs a laugh. "Don't forget I'm still in the room."

"No chance of that," I assure her, sinking into a chair. I managed to come out of the first fight without too many aches and pains, although the back of my neck is stiff from being manhandled and my shins are tender from kicking and checking. "I better not be too long or Seth will come looking for me."

She climbs off Devon, and he gets to his feet and stretches, then he grabs tape and wraps from a bag and hands them over to me. He sits, and I shift my chair around and straddle it, then start on his hands. I can't help dwelling on how much bigger they are than mine, and memories flash through my mind of those fingers on my body, my breasts, or curling inside me as I come. I shiver. His grin hitches up in the corner as though he can read my thoughts.

"You're gorgeous," he whispers. "I love you."

Sucking my lips into my mouth, I don't respond because it's all I can do to focus on wrapping his hands correctly. When I've finished, I turn to Ashlin. "How do you feel about holding pads for him?"

She nods. "I can do that. It's been a while, but I remember how."

"Thanks." I check his wraps, then raise my gaze to his. "I'll be back." Because I can't resist, I brush a kiss over his lips. He lets me retreat without trying for more, and I'm grateful for it.

"Kick some ass, babe," he says as I head for the door. "I'm proud of you."

# Chapter Twenty-Five

*Devon*

The tornado of barely leashed energy within me winds tighter. Soon, it's going to explode. I just hope I can make it into the cage before that happens. It's driving me crazy not having my fight brothers around, and not being able to spend the whole damn night in the same room as Harley. I want to help her prepare, to murmur encouragements in her ear before she goes out for her next two fights.

Fortunately, Ashlin makes it her job to keep me occupied. Seth's ex is sweet, in a quietly competent kind of way. Her mouth is perpetually slanted up at the corners and I can tell how much she cares for Harley. It's in her every word and action. I can't help wondering how my gruff former coach ever wooed her in the first place. She seems like his opposite. Slim, delicate, ethereal—although she holds the pads with strength and calls combinations with a degree of confidence that surprises me.

After I lower my fists and tell her I've had enough, we sit side by side on a pair of chairs and I sip water while she twists a ring on the fourth finger of her right hand.

"So, you and Seth were married?" I ask, because now seems as good a time as any to get answers to questions that no one else is brave enough—or stupid enough—to ask.

"For four years," she replies, continuing to twirl the chunky metal band. "But we were together for three years before that."

"Seven years is a long time to spend with someone."

She sighs, and her hands still. "If you love them, it's nowhere near long enough."

I glance at her, and see that she's staring at a spot on the wall. "You can't make a comment like that and not elaborate."

Giving me a wry smile, she shrugs. "It's not that different from most breakup stories. I loved him, stuff happened, it ended, and it took me years to recover."

"I'm sorry." My gut twists, and I wish I hadn't pried. There's anguish in the depths of her dark eyes that tells me she may not have fully recovered even now.

"Don't be." She sits on her hands, hiding the ring from view. "Just don't break Harley's heart. Whatever happened with Seth and I, she's like a sister to me, and I don't want her hurting."

"You don't need to worry about us," I assure her. "I love her, and I plan to be with her long-term, if she'll have me."

Her phone vibrates, and she checks it. "Harley is on next. Want to head out and watch?"

"Yeah."

We both stand, but before we reach the door, she stops me with a hand on my arm.

"Don't give up on Harley. She can be stubborn, but when she cares, she does it deeply, and I can tell she has strong feelings for you."

"I won't," I promise. "She's it for me, so I've got as much time as she needs."

We take one of the snaking hallways behind the stadium to a rear entrance and slip inside, standing against the back wall to watch. We can't see much from here, but fortunately the action is being streamed onto a number of large screens, and I focus on one of those. I've seen Savage Rose fight a number of times, and she lives up to her name. I have every confidence that Harley can take her down though.

The first round starts, and the two women circle each other. While Harley is relatively unharmed from her earlier fight, Rose is sporting a bruise on the side of her torso and her lip is encrusted with blood. As they exchange blows, neither injury seems to bother her. She pushes forward, trying to drive the action like the pit bull she is, but Harley is magic when she moves. Her striking is effortlessly graceful. Xena, in the flesh. I can't take my eyes off her.

Three rounds later, the final bell sounds and they're both battered and blood-smeared. They bump fists, then sling arms around each other. The crowd goes wild, loving the show of camaraderie. The umpire stands to the side, and we await the decision with bated breath. I think Harley did enough to be crowned winner, but in the absence of a knockout or serious injury, it's almost impossible to be certain. The announcer shouts her name and she launches a fist into the air. Rose nods deferentially, and they hug again before returning to their respective corners.

Beside me, I hear laughter, and turn. Ashlin is watching me with a broad smile.

"Everything I need to know about your feelings for Harley is written all over your face," she says. "You love her."

"I do." I don't care if it's obvious.

"Good." She nods toward the door. "Come on, let's get you ready to go."

---

*HARLEY*

"You were awesome out there." Devon appears in front of me the moment I leave the room reserved for Crown MMA.

I look around, surprised to see him out of his preparation room. "What are you doing here?"

He tucks a lock of hair that came loose in my previous fight behind my ear. "I couldn't wait to see you."

He scans me up and down, but his expression doesn't betray how terrible I look, even though I know it for myself because I checked the mirror. I wiped the blood from my face—some of it being Rose's from a cut at her temple, and some of it mine from a bleeding nose—but there are smears up my arms and spotting on my crop top. On top of that, my eye is turning blue and my right thigh is killing me. All respect to Rose, she was a tough fighter and I'm lucky to have beaten her.

"Is Seth worried about you missing out on down time to help me?" he asks.

"Eh. He'll get over it." Honestly, I think he'd be eager to support Devon himself if not for his whole edict about refusing to train a couple. "Let's get out of here before he comes along. You know he won't be able to stop himself from giving you advice, and we've already worked out your game plan."

A couple of men nod respectfully as I pass, and I return the gesture. It seems Seth's plan is working. I'm gaining the kind of attention that might attract other women to his gym. We arrive at Devon's room, and Ashlin greets us with the gear we need for the fight. A medic is standing beside her, and immediately moves to Devon to give him a once-over and measure his blood pressure before declaring him fit for duty.

"You can do this," I tell him under my breath. "Feeling good?"

He steals a cheek-kiss and grins. "Feeling great. I'm ready to show this asshole what we've got."

An usher arrives and leads us to the arena. Unlike me, Devon took a great deal of care choosing his walk-out song, and the moment it begins, I sense a change come over him. He's focused. His attention is centered on the cage. All of the energy that's usually busting from his seams is carefully directed at the opposition, who is already waiting.

He strides out, with me on his heels. A collective murmur rips around the stadium. Even in this modern time, it's unusual to see a male fighter with a female coach—not that that's what this is, but from the outside, that's how it looks. I can't see Seth, but I can feel his eyes on me. I pretend not to notice, and hope he won't be too hurt that I've recruited Ashlin to help us.

When we reach the base of the cage, someone checks Devon's mouthguard and gloves, then allows him to go up. I stride around the back, waiting for the opportunity to attend to him between rounds. Karson glances over at me, and his eyes widen, but then the umpire speaks to both fighters and the first round begins.

I don't let myself scan the stadium for Seth. It's important for Devon to have every ounce of my concentration right now. While the fighters move, I shout orders. Some he listens to, some he doesn't. I expected nothing less. He may be the man I love, but he's still a loose cannon.

The bell sounds, and Ashlin and I hurry into the cage. While she ices his torso—which has taken a beating from his opponent's shin, I hand him a bottle and brief him on the changes he needs to make if he wants to win.

"Don't try to fight him from a distance," I say. "He thrives on that. You need to get into the pocket and put him on the back foot."

He nods, his eyes wild with adrenaline. "Got it, boss."

The umpire yells for the seconds to get out, and Ashlin and I return to our places. The next round only lasts thirty seconds. Devon crowds Karson, gets him on the ground, and forces him to tap out while the crowd —me included—scream our approval. The umpire raises his hand, and then Devon races down the steps, grabs me around the waist, and spins me in a circle. His mouth finds mine, and we kiss—hot and uninhibited—until he runs out of breath. If the crowd was loud before, it's nothing compared to now.

When he pulls away, I say, "I love you," and watch his eyes light up.

"Back at you, babe." He glances somewhere over my head. Following his gaze, I spot Seth watching us thoughtfully. Ignoring him, I kiss Devon once more. "I want you front and center when I win."

"I'll be there," he promises, and takes my hand as

we head toward the back rooms. He nods to Seth when we reach his side, then he departs, going back to the room with his belongings in it.

"We need to talk later," Seth mutters, the words loud in the quiet corridor. "About you and Dev."

Stopping dead, I pause until he turns to face me. Is this the moment we've been waiting for? I should be happy, but all of a sudden, I'm annoyed at him for holding our futures hostage, whatever his reasons may have been.

"I've been thinking." One of his brows flies up, but that's all the response I get. Undaunted, I carry on. "I love Devon, and whether or not you believe it, we're going to be together for a long time. We work well together, both in and out of the cage, and if you can't find it in yourself to believe in us, I'll seriously have to consider going elsewhere to be with him."

He cocks his head. "You'd do that?"

"Yes." Although the trembling in my chest reminds me I'd rather not. "We're a package deal." Now that I've made the decision, it feels right. I should have done it a long time ago.

He nods once, then returns to walking. I consider pushing the matter, but now isn't the time. I still have one last fight to get through.

"Who's my opponent for the final?" I ask.

"Enya Sears."

Excitement buzzes in my stomach, shoving out the anxiety from our conversation, as I recall the freckled brunette who moves like a ballerina. The one beloved by America, who keeps falling just short of any major win.

*Sorry, Enya. You'll lose again tonight.*

We prepare for the fight in silence, up until the last few minutes, when Seth talks me through his game plan, which is basically to outmuscle her. Enya is technically proficient—I recognized that from seeing her at the Steel Angels—but she isn't powerful.

An usher comes to get us, and I stride to the stadium for the last time tonight. I'm the first one to arrive at the cage, so I shake my limbs to loosen them up. The audience goes bananas when she struts down the aisle. They love her, and I feel a pang of regret that I'm standing between her and the win she so desperately needs. Hopefully she'll be able to pick herself up again when the night is over.

She enters the cage, standing opposite me. I nod to her, and she offers a small smile in return. If not for the bruises decorating her torso and the lump growing on her forehead, she'd look very much like the girl next door. I'm not fooled, though. She's a worthy adversary who made it through two opponents to end up here with me tonight. The umpire calls us to the center, reminds us of the rules, and then the fight begins.

The first round is relatively even. A back-and-forth of exchanges, with each of us taking turns being the aggressor. We're weary from our earlier bouts, and cautious to protect our injuries. She aims a number of kicks at my right thigh, proving that she was watching earlier when it got decimated by Savage Rose.

The second round goes the same way as the first. It's a toss-up as to who's in the lead, and even if Seth hadn't told me in no uncertain terms that I need to up my game, I'd know entering the third round that I need to do something drastic to ensure my success. It's time to leave the comfort zone. Yanking her close, I sweep her off her feet and pin her to the ground. It's the first time I've willingly gone to the floor, but I have more chance of using my strength against her from here. It works well—at first. But then Enya makes a move I haven't prepared for, and all of a sudden I'm the one who's twisted like a pretzel and unsure of the way out.

To my side, Seth is yelling instructions. I try to focus on them, but there's a pain in my arm, and I struggle to breathe. Closing my eyes, I tune out everything except the sound of his voice. My body acts automatically, following his commands, and seconds later, by some miracle, I've reversed our positions. Putting more pressure on her, I up the ante. She thrashes, but thanks to Seth, I've got her in such a good hold, she's unable to break free. Finally, defeated, she taps out.

Stumbling to my feet, I offer her a hand and help her up. She congratulates me, although disappointment is etched in every line on her face.

"Thanks," I reply. "Maybe—"

But then the umpire grabs my arm, and someone shoves a camera in my face. Enya shrugs, as if to say, "what can you do?" then slinks back to her corner.

## Chapter Twenty-Six

*Devon*

I manage to hold off until the promoter climbs the stairs, carrying a bulky belt, before dashing up them myself. The need to congratulate Harley eclipses everything else. She's worked so damned hard for this, and she pulled it off. I don't know many fighters crazy enough to sign up for three bouts in one night, and the crazy in her calls out to the crazy in me.

Slipping an arm around her waist, I kiss her cheek, taking care to avoid any areas that have started swelling. "You did it, Harls. I'm so fucking proud of you." The pride wells up within me, and if I'm not careful, it might spill out my eyes. Wouldn't that be something?

On her other side, Seth claps a hand on her shoulder, his expression full of respect. "You're a badass. Couldn't have asked for anything better."

She smiles hesitantly. "I have the best coach in town."

He looks like he wants to say something else, but the man with the camera has gotten impatient.

Another guy, wearing a suit and tie, asks a question. She answers with a few words, never one to talk for ages, but I don't hear what they are. I'm too distracted by the grin that's transformed her face, and the vitality glowing from her pores. She's so fierce. So alive. It reminds me of when we met, and I took one look at her and believed I was in love. But I didn't know what love is. Not really.

*This* is love. This almost uncomfortably full sensation in my heart, and the knowledge that I'm never going to be completely in control of my life again. The fact that I *like* it, and that, somehow, I think I'll fall in deeper with her every single day, until I don't even recognize my life without her.

Seth catches my gaze behind her back, and tips his head in a nod. I'm not sure what it means, but I like it. The interviewer finishes with Harley, then turns to Seth.

"So, big brother," he says, straightening his tie. "Do you intend to train more female fighters?"

Seth clears his throat and gives the guy his full attention. This is the opportunity he's been waiting for. "I do."

While he goes into a spiel about his plans for the gym, I catalog Harley's features and do an inventory of her injuries. Although her nose was bloodied earlier, it's not too bad. The shiner on her left eye is impressive, and so is the knot on her forehead and the bruise on her thigh. Other than that, she's remarkably fine. Of course, she'll be worn out and have a terrible adrenaline crash, but that's something we expect when we do what we do. It's nothing new.

Moments later, we're leaving the cage, trailing behind Seth toward the exit. A number of men call lewd suggestions to Harley and she gives them the finger. A couple of women yell that she's their new hero, and her spine visibly straightens. I smile. She might not want to believe it, but she has an ego, the same as anyone else in our profession.

As we enter the corridor, Seth drops back to walk with us.

"So." His voice is gruffer than usual from yelling above the roar of the crowd. "Harley threatened to leave the gym to be with you, so you'd better come back."

My heart leaps, and I catch her gaze. "You did?"

I'm scarcely able to believe it. If I'd thought I couldn't possibly love her any more, I'd have been wrong. But the thing is, I suspect she'll be upping the ante every day for the rest of our lives.

She shrugs, as though it's no big deal, when I know that's the farthest thing from the truth. "I love you."

"It wasn't necessary," Seth grumbles. "I already decided I'd made a mistake."

"Thanks, man. You won't regret it." I give him a sly smile. "So, I'm officially your friend again?"

He slides a sideways look at me. "You always were. I missed your crazy ass." He shoves his hands into his pockets. "Mom gave me an earful a couple of days ago. Told me I was wrong to get between you, and now that I can see things more objectively, I have to agree. Also, she approves." He sends a pointed look my way. "So treat Harley with the respect she deserves and don't fuck it up, or I'll revoke your friend status."

"I won't." Then, because it seems like the appropriate man-to-man thing to do, I shake his hand. His grip is firm. Almost crushing. And he stares at me over it. Message received.

"Now," he scans the hall, "I'm overdue for a conversation with Ash."

"Seth, no!" Harley calls after him as he hurries off, but he's a man on a mission. I don't care, because it means I get to be alone with her, and from what I could tell, Ashlin can take care of herself. She may be soft-spoken, but she's no wilting violet.

I grab Harley's hand before she can run after him. "Come on, let's get out of here."

She pauses, clearly torn, but then relents. "He'd better not mess up my friendship."

"He won't," I say, hoping I speak the truth. I'm reasonably sure that Seth knows how to be a decent person, underneath his growliness. I lay a hand on her massive belt. "This looks good on you, but you know where it would look better?"

"Oh, my God." She slaps a hand to my chest. "Do *not* say on the floor."

Winking, I don't say a thing.

She rolls her eyes and groans. "Can't you try to be original?"

I pull her into the shelter of my arms. "How's this for original? I love you more than I love pulling off a perfect uppercut. More than getting Karson Hayes in a rear choke hold. More than—"

She covers my mouth with her hand, her eyes alight with amusement. "I get it." She kisses a line along my jaw before removing her hand. When she does, she holds up a finger, indicating I should let her speak first. "Take me home and put me in a hot bath," she orders. "Then can we snuggle?"

A slow smile curves my lips, and I brush a kiss over her forehead. "I'll snuggle the shit out of you." I thread my fingers through hers, wishing I never had to let go. "Just try to keep up, Isles."

She laughs. "Bring it on, Green."

## Epilogue

*SETH*

Emotions fucking suck.

Mine are a wreck. I feel like a shirt that's been pulled inside out and put in a washing machine on spin cycle. Everything is out of whack and I don't know which way is up. I'm happy for Harley and Devon, but seeing them together reminds me of the gaping hole in my own life where Ashlin isn't. My sister has found someone to share her future with, but I don't have that anymore. I lost my girl, and I don't even know how. It was insidious. Grief ripped us apart from the inside, and neither of us were detached enough from the situation to see it.

I reenter the stadium, and my gaze lands on her immediately, drawn to her like a moth to a flame. It's always been that way with us. I'm the shadow chasing her light. Nipping at its heels and trying to get closer. She shifts her weight, and her hair sways. It's shorter than it used to be, and frames her delicate face perfectly, the deepness of the color emphasizing the paleness of her skin. My own Snow White. Except I haven't been able to call her mine for years.

Time agrees with her. Faint lines cross her forehead and bracket her eyes when she smiles at someone who passes, but they only make her more beautiful. Before I realize it, I'm standing in front of her, and those smile-induced crinkles vanish. She watches me with a coolness I never knew she possessed. My hands clench into fists, and the calluses rub against my fingertips, reminding me that while she's improved with age, I've gotten rougher. I don't bother to shave often, and my face is scruffy as a result. I've added more tattoos to my collection, because what the fuck else am I supposed to spend my money on? I've got no one to spoil and I've never been a person who needed material things or a particular lifestyle.

"I've missed you." As soon as the sentence is out, I cringe. When I see her again in my fantasies, I'm suave and charming, and she realizes how much she wants to be with me, but real life isn't fantasy, and I've never been a man who's good with words. I'm too blunt. Too coarse. She used to love that about me, but now? I know nothing about the woman she's become. She might even be seeing someone.

That thought pierces my heart like a dull blade. I was her first. We got together when she was twenty to my twenty-eight, and she told me she was waiting for the right man to come along. Back then, I took pride in that, but how many men have been with her since because I was too stupid to keep her from slipping through my fingers?

Ashlin's lips firm. They're like perfect little rosebuds, tempting my mouth, but I know better than to give in. "Seth."

227

God, I love the way she says my name. It makes me want to preen beneath her hand like a cat.

She holds my gaze. "I have a proposition for you."

*Hang on a minute. What? That's not how I expected this to go.*

She rubs her lips together the way she does when she's nervous, and suddenly, I'm anxious to hear what she has to say.

"I'm listening."

She glances around, then her gaze darts back to me. "Not here." Her lips rub together again. "Meet me at Sugar. Five p.m. on Wednesday."

Sugar is a café not far from the gym.

"Why can't we talk now?" I ask as my stupid heart hopes and prays that maybe, after all this time, she's rethought our relationship and is willing to give me a second chance.

"Because we need privacy." She tucks her silky hair behind her ear and tilts her face up to mine. "You'll be there?"

I nod. "Wouldn't miss it for anything." But I might die from curiosity in the meantime.

"Good." She touches my shoulder, and even through my shirt, the shock of the contact is enough to make me shiver. "I'll see you then."

"Wait—" I call, but she's already walking away, a swing in her hips that will be imprinted in my mind forever. I've never forgotten anything about Ashlin Isles, and I've never felt even a quarter of what I feel for her for another woman. Seeing her is a sign. What-ever may have come between us in the past, Ashlin is meant to be mine, and I won't let her out of my life again. Not this time.

# Extended Epilogue

*Devon - One Year Later*

I couldn't be more proud as I watch a man the size of a freight train wrap a championship belt around Harley's waist while thousands of people chant her name. The atmosphere in the stadium is electric. Although we're both fighting tonight, she went before me and won her first title bout. Now everyone is speculating whether I'll do the same. We're the reigning power couple in MMA, and I, for one, have my fingers crossed that we'll be heading home with matching accessories. But belts aren't the only thing I have in mind.

Standing to the side, I catch Seth's eye, and he nods. I have his support for what I've planned. Considering he's practically family, it seemed right to talk to him ahead of time. Plus, I need his help.

In the cage, Harley finishes thanking her support team, and when her gaze locks on me and her expression softens, I know her words are all for me. We've got our own language, she and I. She keeps her attention trained on me while she farewells the interviewer, then she saunters down the stairs and launches into my arms. Grinning, I bury my face in the crook of her neck and hold her tight. It took a lot for her to get comfortable enough with me to be so open, and I'll never take it for granted.

"You were amazing out there," I tell her, pulling back so I can kiss her. "You deserved that win, Harls."

Sydney and Lena appear, and group-hug her.

"Guys!" she protests. "I'm sweaty and disgusting."

"You're a queen," Lena says, and I have to agree. Hopefully, soon, she'll be *my* queen.

I take her hand and give them a meaningful look. "Harley is gonna come help me get ready now."

They both beam, and Sydney winks while Harley is busy looking at me.

"Good luck, Dev."

"Thanks, ladies."

As we head toward the exit, Harley murmurs, "We could have stayed with them for longer."

"Maybe," I allow. "But I wanted you to myself for a minute."

"Oh?" Her tone is light, but I'm not fooled. She's intrigued. "And why's that?"

"Because I want you to make me a promise." We enter the room reserved for Crown MMA, which has been emptied thanks to Seth. She doesn't seem to notice, just sits on one of the benches that line the walls. I sit beside her. My stomach is in knots, but I have no doubt. "If I win, you say yes to the next question I ask."

Her brow furrows. "Is it going to be some weird sexual favor?"

I guffaw. If only she knew. "Nope."

Eyes narrowing, she searches my expression for any

hints. "Why should I say yes when I don't know what it will be?"

"Because you trust me," I suggest.

She nibbles her lip, thinking it over.

"Pretty please. Have I ever asked for anything you haven't wanted?"

She rolls her eyes, but the wary purse of her lips softens into amusement. "Okay," she concedes. "But you'd better not make me regret it."

Gleeful, I kiss her cheek. "I won't."

We sit together for another few moments before Seth, Jase, and Gabe rejoin us. This time, I nod to Seth, letting him know we're all go. I have to win this next fight, because my future happiness might depend upon it. I say "might" because there's a good chance she'd say yes regardless of whether I win, but where she's concerned, I'd prefer for it to be a sure thing.

I warm up, and then Gabe takes me through some drills.

When Seth wraps my hands, I lower my voice so I can speak to him without anyone overhearing. "You're sure you're cool with this?"

"Yeah," he answers gruffly. "You're already my brother, Dev. Might as well make it official."

My heart warms but I resist the urge to hug him. He may not be as surly as he used to be, but I doubt he wants me emoting all over him either.

"Thanks, big man."

Shortly after, we head into the stadium again. Harley follows behind, then trails off to sit in the seats reserved for our gym in the front row. I'm facing off against a guy who's relatively new to the States, having come from kickboxing in the Netherlands. He's a scary dude, with more tats than clear skin, but I'm buoyant, and it shows in my performance. Whatever he throws, he can't knock me down. The fight goes right up until the last buzzer. As the umpire stands between us, a whole flock of butterflies stir up my stomach. Did I do enough? Or was I too distracted?

I try to concentrate on the announcer's voice, but all I hear is gibberish. When the umpire raises my hand, I understand that I won. Which means Harley owes me a "yes." The blood is rushing in my ears as the same hulking man who gave Harley a belt brings one to me. He's the promoter for this event. The money behind it. He says something, and I watch his lips move but can't hear anything past the rushing in my ears so I nod and offer him a fist to bump.

Then I spot Seth approaching from the side, his arm around Harley, whose forehead is wrinkled in confusion. They stop in front of me, and Seth reaches into his pocket and hands me a small velvet box. Suddenly, everything crystallizes in startling clarity. The audience murmurs in the background, craning their necks to see what's going on. Harley's breath hitches as I drop to one knee.

"I love you." My voice rings so loud in the hush that I feel like I'm yelling into a speakerphone. "Before I ask you this next question, do you remember the deal we made?"

Understanding dawns, and she nods, and raises a hand to her mouth. "Yes," she whispers, and someone in the distance laughs.

"Not yet, Harls."

Popping the box open, I show her the ring. It's simple white gold, with a single diamond set in the top. Elegant, but not flashy, because she isn't a flashy kind of girl. I swallow, my heart thudding harder than it was five minutes ago, when I was literally engaged in the fight of my career.

"The day I met you, I thought you looked like a warrior princess. I've learned since that there's so much more to you than that, but you're still the queen of my heart." I moisten my lips, hoping like hell she can see all of the emotions I hold for her reflected in my eyes. "Will you marry me, and make it official?"

"Yes," she cries, and reaches down to clasp my free hand and yank me to my feet. The moment she releases me, I curl my arm around her back and draw her in for a kiss. She tastes of something minty. Of warm afternoons in the gym and long evenings snuggled on the sofa. Of tangled sheets and muted sighs. But most of all, she tastes like the future.

She draws away, smiling at me. Radiant. "I love you."

With trembling fingers, I take the ring from the box and hold it up for her to slide her finger into. It's a perfect fit, just like us. The crowd erupts. Forget the fights, this is the loudest they've been all night. For us, and our kickass fairy-tale ending.

"I love you too," I reply softly, just for her. "What say we get out of here and celebrate?"

"That sounds perfect."

I have the urge to sweep her into my arms and carry her out, but my princess doesn't need that. She walks on her own two legs, by my side, of her own volition.

God, I love her. She's my Xena. My muay thai royal.

And I couldn't be happier. Our hands tighten around each other, and we exchange smiles. I know, just *know*, that this is my forever.

### THE END

# Fighter's Second Chance Excerpt

*Seth*

I don't remember the last time I was this nervous. Not when I stepped into the cage for a championship bout. Not even when I got married. Smoothing my hands down my button-down shirt—something I haven't worn in forever—I catch a glimpse of myself in the reflection from the cafe window and wince. I should have shaved. A week's worth of scruff decorates my jaw, with far more silver amongst it than there was back when I was with her.

With Ashlin.

Wiping my sweaty palms on my dark jeans—the nicest pair I own—I glance inside and spot her immediately, at a table in the rear of the cafe, as though she wants to be as far from the other customers as possible. At the sight of her, everything inside me clenches. There was a time when that woman was my entire world. But that was before she sat me down with a homemade dinner and asked for a divorce.

I haul in a breath, straighten my spine, and shove the door open. Inside, the cafe smells of cinnamon buns and pastries. My stomach gurgles, but I dare not put anything in it. I don't know what she wants with me or why she asked me to meet her, but I'm hoping it's for a second chance. There's nothing I want more.

"Ashlin," I say as I stop at her table.

She meets my eyes, every bit as gorgeous as I remember, with delicate pixie features, dark silky hair, and porcelain skin. But where's her smile? Ashlin Isles has a smile for every occasion. At least, she used to. Now, she's cool and reserved as she appraises me. Curling my fingers into my fists, I resist the urge to fidget as I wonder what she sees. I've changed since we were together. I've grown rougher, because it was her influence that smoothed my jagged edges. These days, I rarely glance in a mirror, but I know the crinkles around my eyes have multiplied, and tattoos cover even more of my skin than before—not that she can see them, since the long sleeves and jeans hide the majority.

"Hi, Seth." Her voice is quiet but strong. "Thanks for coming."

"No problem." I pull out the seat opposite her and drop into it. "Want to tell me why we're here?"

A furrow forms between her brows. "Would you like to get coffee first? Something to eat?"

I shake my head. "No, thanks. I'm not hungry."

She nods, and her fingers venture over to the ring finger of her left hand, then pause, and she glances down, as though confused by them. "Do you mind if I do?"

I shrug. "Sure. Go right ahead."

If this is a "let's try again" conversation, I want her to be as comfortable as possible. At the moment, it's plain she's nervous. Ashlin is usually the essence of grace, but every time I catch her eyes, they hold for

236

only a moment before darting away. She waves to a waitress, who comes over, and orders a decaf latte. I raise a brow. Decaf? The Ashlin I knew loved her coffee strong. But then, I haven't seen her for years, so how much do I really know about her these days?

"Good day at the gym?" she asks while we wait for her drink to arrive.

"Same as usual." I've been running Crown MMA Gym for eight years, since before we divorced—before we were married, as a matter of fact. But she was there in the very beginning, encouraging me to pursue my dream because we both knew that my time as a professional MMA fighter was limited. No matter how good I was, age catches up with everyone. Becoming head coach at my own gym was a retirement plan. Now here I am, with one of the best gyms in the country, but no wife to share my success.

"Devon is back at training?" she asks.

I nod. "Dangerous" Devon Green has recently returned to the gym after a brief stint away while I came to grips with his relationship with my baby sister. I was worried about them at first since they effectively had a workplace romance, but fortunately, it seems to be working out. I'll never hear the end of it for going overprotective big brother on their asses.

"Yeah. He is."

"How do you feel about that?"

"I wish they'd gone about things differently," I confess. It had taken them God knew how long to come clean with me. Am I really such a scary guy that my sister and one of my closest friends couldn't be honest from the beginning? "I'm not upset about them as a couple though. They'll be good for each other."

"I think so too," she says. Her drink is delivered, and she takes a sip, then clasps it between her hands as if to warm them, even though it's a balmy eighty degrees out. "Right." She takes a breath. "I suppose I should get to the point."

"That would be great. I've got no idea what I'm doing here."

She nods, then meets my eyes and holds the connection. "I want to have a baby."

"*What?*" I gasp for air as the metaphorical floor falls out from under me. No blow I've ever received from an opponent could knock me down the way she has with one statement.

I was there the last time she got pregnant. I witnessed the emotional aftermath of our miscarriage. Hell, I lived it. She fell apart, went through a period of depression, and I couldn't do anything to help. Why would she want to put herself through that again?

She continues to hold my gaze. For all that she's delicate and sweet, Ashlin is steely when it counts. "I still want children, and after all this time, I'm finally strong enough—body and mind—to have them."

I want to protest. She didn't see herself after we lost Cara. My thumb goes instinctively to the small tattoo inside my wrist. Our daughter's name. I rub it back and forth, soothing myself, trying to ward off a wave of helplessness brought on by the memories. Ashlin had vanished into herself, and I disappeared into work. Then everything I cared about came crumbling down. But on the heels of the old grief comes something else.

*Jealousy.*

"I didn't know you were seeing anyone." Why is she even telling me this? Some kind of misguided attempt to prevent me getting hurt if I were to learn about it later? Too late. I wanted to grow old with her. To raise a family. It was one thing when I thought she just didn't want that anymore because it was too much for her to handle, but to know she wants it with someone other than me is just cruel.

"I'm not." She sighs, and glances down for a second. Long enough for me to know she isn't comfortable with this conversation. "I'm going to do it by myself."

"Wait, what?" She remembers how pregnancy works, right? Man + Woman + Sex = Baby. I'm not sure how she intends to remove the male part of the equation.

She rolls her eyes. "IVF. I'll go through a fertility treatment and impregnation process. After the damage from our miscarriage, it's my best chance of success."

"No man involved?" I clarify.

"Well, actually…" She bites her lip. "I need a donor. I was going to choose one from a catalog, but none of them felt right."

My jaw drops. Choose a father for her baby from a goddamn catalog? Of all the crazy ideas. Of course it didn't feel right. It's stupid.

"You're the only man I can imagine as the father." She swallows, and her throat bobs. "I know it's a lot to ask, but will you consider it? Will you help me have a baby?"

---

*Ashlin*

They can probably hear my heart beating the next county over. Shock is written across Seth's face, and etched in the clench of his jaw. A vein throbs at his temple. I fight the urge to yell "Punked!" and run for the exit. I knew he'd be surprised, but I've spent weeks dwelling on my choice, and haven't approached him

239

lightly. Right now, securing his agreement is the single most important thing in my universe, so I don't flinch when he curses. I don't glance down, or give him any indication that I'm not a hundred percent sure of my decision.

I am unwavering.

"Do you really think getting pregnant is a good idea?" he asks, the grooves around his mouth deepening.

I inhale slowly to buy myself a moment of calm. I knew this question would come, and I'm prepared for it. "I can understand why you'd ask that, considering what I put us both through last time, but I've been in therapy and it's really helped." One of my hands trembles, so I rest the other on top of it. "I'm ready to try again."

"Ash…" That vein continues to throb at his temple. "Are you sure? Perhaps your memory of the time after the miscarriage is fuzzy, but for me, it's crystal clear. You weren't okay. And I… I let you down. Wasn't there when you needed me. I'll always regret that, and I'm not sure if I can be part of something that puts you at risk again."

My stomach sinks, even though I understood this was a possibility. I force my shoulders to stay back. Time to preserve my dignity.

"If you don't want to be involved, that's fine, but you should know that I'm going ahead anyway."

His eyes widen, and he flinches almost imperceptibly. "Still so fucking stubborn," he mutters.

He looks down at his hands, turning them over and studying his palms. I follow his gaze, ignoring the flash of warmth that travels through me. They're large and rough, and even though it was years ago, I remember with perfect clarity how they felt on my naked body.

He used to touch me as though I was precious, but the more he lost control, the less care he took, and I reveled in his wildness.

"Just tell me something." He squeezes his hands into fists and raises his eyes, anger flaring in their blue-green depths. "Why the fuck do you want to hurt yourself this way?" He starts to reach for me, but then stops and drags in a slow breath. When he continues, his voice is like sandpaper. "I don't want to see you in pain."

Oh, God. It's just like it used to be. He's a great, unsettled beast of a man that needs taming, and I want to stand behind him and soothe him with my hands the way I used to. Run them down his shoulders and back. Kiss the side of his neck. Watch the tension ease from him. My body clenches with the effort it takes not to go to him. I didn't realize that his magnetism would be so potent after all this time. I should have known better. Whatever our problems, Seth and I have always been attracted to each other to the point of insanity.

"It's okay," I reassure him. "I can handle whatever comes." I might not enjoy it, but I can survive. Of this, I'm certain. "I want a family, and I'm strong enough to fight for one. Like I said, if you'd rather not be involved, that's fine, but I'm doing it anyway."

His eyes narrow. Oh, he doesn't like that. Of course he doesn't. There was a time when I'd cave in to nearly anything he wanted if he used that gruff, bossy tone of his. But I'm not budging on this. His jaw shifts as he resists the urge to spill out the first response that pops into his head. Despite the circumstances, I have to smile. Always a hothead.

"I can give you time to think about it," I say, beginning to rise from my chair. "I know it's a serious decision."

"No." He gestures for me to stop. "Sit." I do. He rolls his shoulders up to his ears and back down again. "I want to help. I can't fucking stand the idea of seeing you pregnant with another man's kid."

He knows there would be no touching involved, right?

Still, a thrill shoots through me at his possessiveness. We're not together anymore, and perhaps I need to have my head examined, but I always loved the way he made it clear who I belonged with and warned off anyone else. It made me feel cherished. Adored. Sternness aside, Seth Isles is capable of making a woman feel like a siren and a princess all in one.

I stay quiet, waiting.

"Okay." His shoulders heave as the word leaves him on a rush of air. Those gorgeous turquoise eyes meet mine, and my insides tumble over each other. "I'll do it."

"Thank you." It feels like I've been holding my breath forever, and finally released it. I meant it when I said I'd go ahead with or without his help, but it wouldn't have felt right. Choosing candidates from a list of physical attributes and places of employment seems cold. Distant. Especially when I've spent months picturing a perfect little baby with Seth's crystal eyes and my dark hair.

Discomfort worms its way into my gut. Part of me is afraid that all of this is my subconscious's method of bringing him back into my life, but I shut that little voice down. I'm strong enough to stand on my own two feet. I've been doing it for three years now. I've proved to myself that I'm resilient and capable. So what if Seth makes my pulse climb and my heart soften? It doesn't mean anything.

"You won't regret it." I reach for my bag and

extract a sheath of papers, then pass them to him. "This is a legal contract that sets out how everything will work."

He baulks, glancing from the papers to me, and back again, his distaste apparent. "Is that really necessary?"

"Yes." Of this, I'm certain. I won't allow any shades of gray. "Read it later. Have your lawyer look at it. Whatever you need."

"I'm sure it's fine." He sets the papers aside and props his chin on his hand. "Let me pay for the procedure. IVF is expensive, right?"

I shake my head. "I have enough in my savings. It's important to me that I pay myself."

"Are you sure?" I can tell he wants to argue. He thinks he's protecting me by taking on a financial burden, but I know the truth: I have to prove that I can stand on my own. I *need* it.

"Yes." I raise my chin, waiting to see how he reacts.

To my surprise, he nods. "If that's what you want."

# Also by A. Rivers

### Crown MMA Romance

*Fighter's Heart*

*Fighter's Best Friend*

*Fighter's Secret*

*Fighter's Second Chance*

### Crown MMA Romance: The Outsiders

*Fighter's Frenemy*

*Fighter's Fake Out*

*Fighter's Mercy*

*Fighter's Forever*

### King's Security

*The King*

*The Veteran*

# Acknowledgments

First of all, a big thank you to Sheridan, Evie, and Laura for beta reading *Fighter's Secret* and helping me tighten some important points. My editor (the lovely Serena) said it might be my favorite of hers that she's read (a statement that was only followed by a few paragraphs of things to fix rather than pages, woo!). On that topic, thank you to Serena for your ongoing support with this series, and to Kate for polishing the rough edges off. Maria, I love the cover you designed for me. Publishing these books really is a team effort.

Thanks to a certain fighter I used to train with. I didn't even realize that your 'give no shits, no holds barred' approach to fighting (and life in general), and your roguish charm underpinned so much of Devon's character until it came time to write these acknowledgements. Now I see it was there all along.

Last, but definitely not least, a heartfelt thank you to my husband. Your ongoing support and willingness to feed the dog when I forget that meal time is a thing is what keeps my world turning. I count myself so lucky to have someone like you who encourages me to pursue my dreams.

# About the Author

A. Rivers writes romance with strong heroes and heroines who kick butt and take names. She loves MMA fighters, investigators, military men, body-guards, and the protective guy next door who isn't afraid to fight the odds for love.

Printed in Great Britain
by Amazon